Paul's Case
The Kingston Letters

Paul's Case
The Kingston Letters

Lynn Crosbie

a misFit
b o o k

INSOMNIAC PRESS

Edited by Michael Holmes/a misFit book
Copy edited by Lloyd Davis & Liz Thorpe
Designed by Mike O'Connor

Canadian Cataloguing in Publication Data

Crosbie, Lynn, 1963 -
    Paul's Case

Includes bibliographical references and index.
ISBN 1-895837-09-X

1. Bernardo, Paul - Fiction.   2. Homolka, Karla - Fiction.
I. Title.

PS8555.R61166P28 1997   C813'.54   C97-931375-9
PR9199.3.C6893P28 1997

Printed and bound in Canada

The publisher gratefully acknowledges the support of the Ontario Arts Council.

Insomniac Press
378 Delaware Ave.
Toronto, Ontario, Canada, M6H 2T8

CONTENTS

There are also postcards :

PREFACE

This is a critical enterprise, an exploration of the crimes of Paul Bernardo and Karla Homolka as a work of historical fiction. Works of imaginative investigation, these "letters" are not intended as truth claims. They are, however, designed to explore and invent a series of conjectures, to tell the truth, in Emily Dickinson's words, *slant*.

References to persons living and dead are purely fictional, and designed as imaginative and analytical responses to extant portraits of these individuals.

This book is dedicated to my father, with love.

A Good Deal of the Incidental Symbolism

For their betrayal of humanity, (murderers) deserve no better fate than to be permanently excised from the social order. Their only value is as objects of study.
— Elliott Leyton

I made you
and take you made
into me.
— Audre Lorde, "Recreation"

And we are in hell, and a part of us is always in hell, walled-up, as we are, in the world of evil intentions.
— Gaston Bachelard

His lips were continually twitching...Paul was always smiling, always glancing about him, seeming to feel that people might be watching him and trying to detect something.
— Willa Cather, "Paul's Case"

I feel as though I have been sold or pledged myself to the devil.
— Leopold von Sacher-Masoch

People. I know I've done some really terrible things, I know that. And I've caused a lot of sadness and sorrow to a lot of people, and I'm really sorry for that and I know I deserve to be punished...
— Paul Bernardo

MAP

KEY

I've done some terrible things…

1. FEAR

Paul Bernardo
Kingston Penitentiary
King Street West
Kingston, Ontario
K7M 2E7

We shall therefore star the text, separating, in the manner of a minor earthquake, the blocks of signification of which reading grasps only the smooth surface…
— Roland Barthes, S/Z

You, reader, know the delicate monster.
— Baudelaire

August 27, 1996

Dear Paul,

I was in Fire Island the day the verdict was announced. I hadn't seen the Atlantic since I was nine years old. Then, I would run in right away. My first taste of salt, the ocean tossing me up. I swam like a shark, tireless and blind. When I arrived, David and Ira brought me to the beach. They dove into the surf with bright red boards. I hesitated, then moved in slowly, feeling the undertow shift the sand. The water darkened, crested, and knocked me over. When I tried to stand up I was pulled under and thrown into another wave. I ran, choking and falling, to the shore, and wouldn't go back.

The first day of September. You were pronounced guilty of nine charges: two counts each of first-degree murder, kidnapping, forcible confinement and aggravated sexual assault, and one count of committing an indignity to a human body. Your wife, Karla Homolka, was already serving time for two counts of manslaughter — twelve years for her role in the murders of Leslie

Mahaffy, Kristen French, and Tammy Homolka.

I had followed the trial. The composite pictures of the Scarborough Rapist (who turned out to be you). The disappearance and discovery of two teenage girls: one found in a lake, cut into pieces and placed in concrete blocks, the other found naked in a ditch with her hair cut off. Both of them raped and beaten. The arrest of Homolka. The deal she cut to testify against you before the videotapes were found. Your arrest. The discovery of video-tapes, films of these girls. Your trial, which I attended, shaking, because I did not know what I would feel when I saw you both.

Feeling nothing, watching Homolka testify. Watching the back of your head. Nothing.

Leaving for New York as the jury deliberates, arriving at Fire Island. The woods are dry and brittle. There has been no rain and there are caution signs in the laneways: fire. That night we walk the dog on the beach and he finds a crab-shell. When he shakes it seven baby crabs fall out.

We wrench it from his mouth and they creep into the darkness. The sky is red and orange, burning.

I am staying in a stranger's study, behind the house. It is designed like a ship-captain's room; small and unventilated. I look up at a school assign-ment tacked to the wall. For a creative writing course. Write a List Poem, it says. There are examples, involving tangerines, lemons, pomegranates and blackberries. I see that I am bleeding: squadrons of mosquitoes have appeared, vectorial. I can't sleep and I try to write — why do I always feel this way I can't stay here I can't — a list poem:

> Fire Island
> Pitch black, pitched back
> Unlocked window, killers
> Vampire bugs; crabs' legs
> Tinderbox, seething
> Sleepless, Fear

I am thinking of murder and I run back into the main house and leave the lights on. I wasn't thinking about you, I hadn't heard. I had to call to find out. Men who look through windows, who have wanted me dead. I had stopped sleeping months before.

There were things I wanted to say, about the way I felt, about how little I felt until I would begin. Afraid and appalled. Wanting to face you.

Ira took my arm the next day. He pulled me out past the breakpoint. One wave fell, and crashed around me. I left this water, feeling safe. And blessed and other things I had forgotten.

Crumpled miserably on the bed the day I went under. David sat with me and read a poem by Anne Sexton. About a time she was scared in the ocean and ran away. It was the end of the poem he wanted me to listen to, and now I'm writing to you, listening:

> There is no news in fear
> but in the end it's fear
> that drowns you.

You showed no signs of remorse, I would read. There is no news in that; your remorse doesn't concern me. I have been anxious about myself, what is missing. Intent on invention, I am writing you a letter in fifty-two sections. Simple cartomancy between a young fair-haired man who is the Jack of Spades, a young dark-haired woman who is the Queen of Clubs. Interfaced, I will assist you, although you are dangerous, and not worth the effort. According to the *Little Book of Fortune Telling*.

Which also suggests that you attach small stars to the cards. These stars are useful when, arranged in an archway, the cards *begin to contradict each other*.

(These patterns are referred to as The Doors — you know the day divides the night, night divides the day).

You can shuffle and cut these letters, crayon them with constellations. Peculiar combinations will foretell misfortune, death, the assistance of friends.

Or play fifty-two pickup. Just throw them in the air and gather them randomly. Stacking love on injury, on fear and mystery. This is up to you: a way to pass your time. Fold, spindle and mutilate them; make an exquisite corpse. A picture we will draw together, oblivious of each other's intentions.

This letter begins again with an aside. It could be meaningful: *a woman you do not know well has deceived you. She is trying to hide this from you.*

The rest follows: A woman of ill repute who is disheartened, and curious: Beware of her. She is not fond of you.

Silence is usually the preferable surrounding for the reading of cards.

Sharin Morningstar Keenan died the year I came to Toronto. She was a little girl and her killer is still out there. His name is Dennis. He raped and strangled her, left her in his refrigerator. The neighbours heard the noise, but were too frightened to call for help. He is balding, a large man with broad features. He is missing part of one of his fingers; at bars, he arranges his loose coins in a circle around his glass. I think about them both, now and then. Of seeing him and calling the police, while nailing his hands to a table with ice picks. Of her, without fetish, though her small body bends like a swan against the metal racks. I think of how terror is consumed. As if she is a python, swallowing an elephant. I will imagine her parents, a mother's head crowned in peacock feathers, painting a mandala around her navel: morningstar. Her father who shuffles through dim hallways at night, listening.

The killer's hair is thin and dark. He fills me with disgust; and she, beatified, has risen. Her cygnet limbs streaming, beyond my sight. Even so, I think of him more often, with great agitation. The two-boned digit rapping against formica, his corona of coins: clues. I think of his father, torturing him, and try to envision an illness I cannot occupy. But understand in small stabs. The desire, as an adult, to inhabit two subject positions. At one time, you were defiled and powerless: the tall shadow of the monster, the way you curled into a ball and waited for the blows. When you inflict these blows on others later, it is a lot like acting. There is this and simple cruelty. A thrill, like stepping, simply, from a ledge. Your carelessness supports you. Falling with a rattle to the ground, you rise. And perversion. A sick sensation, like swooning: our entire capacity. You want to throw up when you think about it, your breath becomes shallow. Forcing your tongue through a child's kiss, laying bare and breaking the covenant. Innocence makes you ill and angry.

Dennis is overweight and has a wide sloping forehead. He is not visible. It has been over ten years and he is sitting somewhere now, feeding money into a jukebox until "Summer Wind" drops into place. His eyes close in revery: two sweethearts (I live just across the park — be quiet be quiet be quiet) and the summer wind.

I lost you, he thinks, or doesn't. But still the days live on and on, and I need to know you. Pieces of my own life lost in you: *Just stand still and be quiet.* A girl's eyes narrowing, white slits. Thick fingers closing them, with coins.

> *If one calls bricolage the necessity of borrowing one's concepts from the text of a heritage, which is more or less coherent or ruined, it must be said that every discourse is bricoleur.*
> — Jacques Derrida

By now you've stopped reading Paul (*tacco et video*); you have torn this letter to shreds or let it slide to the floor, more or less coherent or ruined. You are tired all the time. I followed your trial closely, in my own way. *Bricolage.* Some makeshift repair of the event, clippings I kept close at hand: I Was Enjoying Myself, Sir.

Newspapers I cut out and stapled together randomly, their headlines like pulp paperbacks I have always wanted to own (*Make My Bed in Hell*). I have made you over with these materials, differently. A lurid flipbook — Paul jumps from Hawaii to prison in one deft shuffle — inured to you, I touch your picture, goodbye, when I leave this desk to buy one pint of milk/sugar/envelopes. Think of setting you on fire, tarred and feathered, a soiled dove. Return, disgusted, and withdraw the sheaf of yellowing packrat papers, absent-mindedly folding them into shapes. A sugar cone; a grass pyre; a burial shroud.

I look around for something you like, thinking how obtuse you are, how you lie. Beyond good and evil, in a region that is simulated. (You watched *Wall Street* to discover, *And when you gaze long into an abyss the abyss also gazes into you,* then pasted this aphorism to your wall).

If Nietzsche was an invalid and his Fascist sister re-arranged his work for her own purposes, he never meant to say *Te amo* Mussolini, Hitler, *liebling*.

He may have heard the gunshot; delirious, he may have seen the hanged body, burned and mutilated, swaying. At the end of his rope, he thought of woman's nature, her capacity for revenge: *the tiger's claws beneath the glove and inner savagery. This dangerous and beautiful cat woman.*

He refers to me as a *beast of prey*, when I borrow from him also, and asks that I do not erase the line, but examine each region. An orthographic projection that reveals hidden points and corners. I am cornering you, and I am getting closer, closer than I was when I came to your trial. When I wrote to you in January and asked you to explain something to me. I detest your crimes, I said, parenthetically. But I know that you have been punished To The Full Extent Of The Law.

My flower of evil, hypocrite Lector:

Comme d'autres par la tendresse,
Sur ta vie et sur ta jeunesse,
Moi, je veux régner par l'effroi.

You see that I have made a girl of you and you are afraid. In French everything is gendered, my glue, *chérie*, darling scissors: a scissoresse, sorceress. You liked to cut and paste things too, I read; and it was disgusting, you said, dismembering a corpse. Locked in antitheses and disinterested, in what makes things work. I wrote a nice polite letter to you without spelling errors (it occurs to me I have never taken a clock or a radio apart) and you didn't write back. That was something like love, what I have known in the past. Reaching out, and my beloved recoils. Dogs get killed that way, trying to get away from you. You tend to make people uneasy, revolted. What — was I saying? I know that you are barely alive, that your partner is almost through. It is possible that I should be writing to her. But she is not the captive audience I require.

She does love to read so it's unfortunate. Karla enjoys mysteries; her IQ is formidable. When she is not busy with her schoolwork, she devours true-crime novels. Please send me that book about the Monsters of the Moors, she wrote to a friend. Twice, on flower-bordered paper, perfumed with Poison

a potion in plum-coloured glass   Myra Hindley's atomizer of Tabu.

Myra also killed children, and she kept things clean and simple. A striking blonde in black; Ian Brady photographed her, in high boots and mesh stockings. Long red nails shining, whiphand. Riding on the back of his Triumph, her arms wrapped around his waist, screaming Faster, and while he dug the graves she walked out farther in the mist. She looked up at what moon there was, milky above the scrim of her long lashes. She has since become a model prisoner and her tastes are no longer catholic; her lips move carefully, with humility,

at mass (bodies of matter of indefinite shapes).

Martha Beck and Raymond Fernandez, an obese nurse with a gigolo husband who practiced voodoo (the dead walk the earth). Executed for multiple murders on March 9, 1951, Beck remarked that theirs was a love story that only those tortured by love could understand. Tortured by Love. This is a misprision, which Karla would recognize, shifting the words around into a more logical sequence.

Folie à deux: a clinical term for the lunacy or madness of one and another. These four and you two make three. As an accountant, surely you understand the figures. You are not like anyone else either, please don't misunderstand me.

I do not want to confuse you any further, although I was wondering if you think of weakness and strength in adversative terms. Because I will examine you, with affection and loathing, bend and break you.

The play within this play is performed with shadow puppets: as Minerva, I call out to you in a thin and ruthless voice, Hades, leave your dark realm and show yourself.

This morning I thought about heaven, that it is not an assembly but a retreat into dreams. Dreams I write unbidden, within a traversal, the milky way between each hemisphere. John Rosen, your lawyer, showed Karla a photograph of her sister's dead body and she looked away. Look at it, he commanded. This satisfied many, though I will carve out her eyes instead. She has become the blonde starlet of my Senecan drama. Like Vendice (and you my Gloriana), I'll make the bad bleed and the tragedy good.

Deploying stichomythia, repeating and opposing myself, repulsing you. Speaking all the while in inherited tropes: falling angels, the spherical cycle of violence and consolation. I'll be the entire chorus, sliding across the stage in strophe, antistrophe, and epode, standing still. Just looking at you again as I have and will, your immutable face the place you reside: where no birds sing. I visited the Kingston Penitentiary last Sunday, walking past the gun towers, sensors and guards. Toward the lake, passing by your little window, toward you. Sitting on your mattress, one foot is hooked beneath you as you fold and refold a towel.

The sun razing the water, the rotunda of silver and gold. You heard me approach, as you did in court last July when I was late and dressed like an assassin. Detained by the police, I had just arrived when you were led through the door. In a forest green suit and tie (paler bars of green), your head averted, from me.

I could see your mouth moving, your lips pulling at the corners. It's that tremor that gives you away, that would arouse my suspicion, if you had ever asked me to accompany you to your car or hotel room in Fort Lauderdale. Maybe feeling good, the sand circled from the rim of a tequila glass leaving olympian symbols, the lost weekend inflamed with your profile or poetry: *Poor soul, the centre of my sinful earth.* My body still pale but burning, watching your mouth calculate how easily my arms can be bound behind my back, the crack of the blade (dislocation occurs when the arm is abducted). But I was never young. Waiting always, looking at the prim curve of your white collar, the tenderness of your neck. Still against the bulletproof glass, even my eyes which

Like comets shine through blood

you resist. Laughing once with your lawyer (the lesser one, who still fields calls), pulling at his robes in a gesture of contempt while he play-hits you and you shrink. And shaking your head when Karla says, Ask Paul. He knows the truth.

Already this letter has become intimate. I have included an appendix because this is all so factual and specific and does not flow like lyrical fiction: gibson riverrun, past paul and karla. The surfeit of information and documentation has freighted my imagination: it is sinking, like a cement casket, into the mud and green water of the serpentine stream.

The prose is inelegant. What I mean is it is prosaic, the way you try to speak.

Also I am overdressed: white lab coat, stethoscope, book-strap, pick axe, magnifying glass, fossil-brush, latex gloves, razors, black hood. I could write a horrifying poem about you: I am stabbing you over and over and you will not die. Something detached, or smooth true-crime: The sun burned unusually bright that day, although Port Dalhousie residents would remember feeling a chill in the air. I could pin you down and dissect you, or care for you in my own nervous illness. Split your atoms in a chamber, tear you to shreds until I am greeted

avec des cris de haine

(Burn in Hell You Bastard).

Instead I will examine each element. There is no consolation in elegy: I have not been well. When the ambulance arrived there was smoke everywhere. The policeman reached out to me and held my hand, examining the incisions. He asked, Do you want to come with me?

Revision — writing redemption, benedictions, untruth. In dejection, I have turned to you: come with me.

Because I have so many questions, because you have nothing else to do. Unfolding, then folding the towel into shapes: a triangle, a sailor's hat, a crescent moon. There is a woman who visits you, who compares herself, with some indignation, to a nun. She mentions her Bible, how she sticks it with pins and counsels you, swings low singing the Song of Solomon as you bow your head and your kiss, remembered, is sweeter than wine. You have mentioned, unsuccessfully and in your own defence, how film is often imported into life; you have tried to unravel deceptions: you have failed. I suggest to you that, like me, your little nun knows a dead man walking when she sees one. Things have a habit of reverting to form, a square, a stone, an apron.

Among the many things you said in court: that you did not beat and throw Karla into a mud puddle; that Kristen French's last words were not

"There are some things worth dying for." Among the things you did not say: that Homolka is a grifter, who borrowed much of her testimony from television, books, and film. Paul knows the truth, she said on several occasions, nodding at you. *Toronto Sun* posters all over the city during the trial: your face framed with the legend THE TRUTH THE WHOLE TRUTH.

(My mistress's eyes, you remarked & I hold this picture now, looking into yours).

If you could be more logical in the assembly of your ideas they might acquire a critical contour, the edges of the towel gathered to produce *Illuminations*.

Your opponent is dangerous, one who told the police you were too stupid to hold onto someone captive; one who was playing with a Hardy Boys crime-fighting kit (matching her prints with those of Alice Crimmins, Mary Flora Bell, Diane Downs) while you were walking silently through your Scarborough home, staring into space.

You did not speak until you were five, merely pointed and grunted, a fact which your lawyer did not mention. By the age of two and a half the average child has at least a 200-word vocabulary. If he does not, he may develop a grimace or facial twitch. He may be hearing or speech impaired; or he may be *giving his concentration and energy to acquiring some other skill.*

While the lack of oxygen in your brain during your birth is thought to have caused this protracted aphasia, your speaking skills, curiously, developed in direct correlation to your skill as a voyeur (creeping under night windows as a boy, your hands crossed over your pants, listening for Eros's first snap and click). Your father preoccupied, more interested in girls, gentle with them, easing their skirts up, navigating. Rosen, like the Metro Police, forgets to extract your DNA from the electrophoresis gel; he does not see the way its strands bend, in small pirouettes.

He's not my real father, you would say. Your mother claims to have had an affair. You think of her as a whore. And wonder about what is learned, what is encrypted (The Bad Seed).

Karla dressed in pink and white, her blonde hair loose as she hung out the window to see the hamster fall to the lawn. Alight on the wind, bound to a pillow case, it tumbled to the grass, stunned.

She loved dolls and admonished children who killed insects.

Encountering a child in a schoolyard with tiny arms (which ended like flowers where elbows should be), she cornered the girl's brother and said his sister was a freak, a seal who belonged in the zoo; creepy looking, is what she called her, as she combed her doll's yellow hair.

After the hamster died, she dug it up to look at it, sepulchral with maggots and worms, its limbs rigid, gesturing to the stars. I'm going to be famous, Karla said.

You are standing in a schoolyard also, smiling. As a group of
children surround you in a circle. Calling *barnyard barnyard*
what a smelly barnyard. You cried and wondered
why is everyone so mean to me?

Learning fast to meet evil with evil: "Out of every adversity comes the seed of an equal or greater benefit." One of many quotations you organized in columns along your bedroom wall.

It's just evil, writing to you this way.

Someone wrote this graffiti on newspaper boxes all over the city: Stop Profits From Bernardo. In black.

I don't know if you know this, but people hate your guts. Your best friend keeps ratting you out and collecting money. He was devoted to you (although he always thought there was *something unusual* about you).

One woman saw your lookalike in an advertisement for a CD player and went nuts, writing to magazines. The whole thing pains me, she said.

Or someone will say, out of the blue: He has a television in his cell. It's disgusting.

Sometimes I wonder if you're watching the same thing I am.

When I'm alone and hear strange noises: the gang in the alley (known as The Apostles). I worry about things. I have worried your case like a handkerchief. All the loose ends.

My doubt is reasonable, passed on to you on azure sheets of paper, with a black rat insignia. Slinking through the events of your trial, drawn to the smell of what is concealed, possibilities. Putrefaction.

Suspicion, torments my heart. I sing to you, when I remember —
I heard the defence attorney yell, This is the face of a killer! Pointing to
a frozen video frame. Spectators were not able to see these images. I imagine
you looked furious, your features contorted with rage.

Not at all benign. The way you looked when you came to the stand and
waved your arms expansively. People, you said. I've done some terrible
things. But I did not kill these girls.

Killers look very angry and ugly. They should always begin their testimony by impersonating a politician. Their attorneys should never, under
any circumstance, introduce relevant psychiatric evidence.

Killers are not pretty. When Karla took the stand, she was lovely.
Exceptionally polite and well-groomed. I want Paul to drool when he sees
me, she said.

Pretty girls are not killers. Please pass me a tissue. Thank you. Yes sir,
that is the truth, Paul killed them all, I have never hit anyone in my life. I
merely stopped my sister's breath.

No I cannot explain why the victim had small knee cap-shaped bruises
on her back, or why her face was bruised. It is true that Paul didn't hit her,
but I never used that mallet. I've never hit anyone in my life! Yes I am
aware that women invariably strangle with a ligature, not their bare hands. I
suppose it makes it easier for them, but what you are proposing is a lie. Paul
used that ligature, ask him.

May I be excused? Thank you.

The semiotics of women and violence: THE GUN WENT OFF, SHE
STOPPED BREATHING.

The spectre of Lizzie Borden: Just look at this woman. Does she look like
a murderer?

I think about these things and write them down. I am writing you an
essay. It is experimental, analagous to your case. Your sex trial, where female
sexuality was never mentioned. An experiment involving burial and decom-
position, the essence that attracts rats who mistake it for perfume.

Paul, you are a sick and hateful man but you might as well be dead. Even
if you aren't a murderer, you'll never see the light of day. The light of day
you once watched breaking through the blinds and illuminating Karla's
beautiful face.

The same sun that rose as she lay in a psychiatric ward, nodding on anti-psychotics, anti-depressants and tranquilizers. Enthralled by the attention, her doctor, Mesmer, drawing out untruths from the point of a needle.

While you languished, unexamined. Withholding your pathologies, all this deviance stonewalled: this cat has your tongue.

Pretty cat, who had her wrists slapped after playing rock paper scissors: the long arm of the law covered her briefly, a white sheet on a stone.

(I would never write to Karla because she might write back.)

I only mention all this because I have talked about these letters to a friend. He was disquieted although he liked all the mean things I said I would write, especially the part about sticking a knife right down your throat. But so does anyone who saw the Stones live, playing Midnight Rambler. Right here in Toronto at the El Mocambo — on that recording some girl screams Paint it Black. Paint it Black, You Devil.

Just like my friend.

I cannot erase your baby's face with black marker any more than I can Love You Live. You're doing something dangerous, he said. And I said, coldly, as I left, Danger Is My Business.

To return home and feel ashamed. And wish I was the avenger he wants me to be. The contract killer, the girl who was frightened of you my whole life.

Maybe you have read the three books about you, though I doubt it. I mean, I don't think you're allowed to read pornography in jail. This is irony, which you may or may not know. I have read them all and I'm tired of the story. It never changes, and I want to mix things up with you.

You will become confused and uncertain. Never knowing who I am. All of these voices and false/true documents. As if you are in court again, drawing question marks on a legal pad. Or worse, as if you are desperately unhealthy: you have begun imagining things. Everything I am asking you to absorb or swallow.

Because you don't say a word your purpose is certain. A cold seed, unhooked from its nidus, a pure object of study. Your value, however, cannot be determined. Unearthing you, I may discover what you have entombed (archaeologists hold up ropes of jewels, stepping over the bodies of the sentries, buried alive); I may stand, filled with fear, in a derelict cave. Where bats whisper and cling, high among the charred rocks and cold stalactites.

Either way, I will present you in fragments. And make a figment of you. With one bone or sunken footprint, scientists have built killers: I see them, as I think of you, in the golden light of the museum, craning their vicious heads as if advancing. When I draw away, I see the wooden ligatures and pegs, their hollowed eyes. They are harmless, but I have never moved closer, to touch them.

2. Blond Van in a Beige Camaro

The following is a chapbook that is currently being circulated in Toronto. It is a work of fiction.

Saturday

Took more scrapings from Paul today. He was hanging onto the window-sill in one of his trances. While he swayed back and forth, staring at something in the window, never through the window. Why? Who looks at a window? I quickly drew a letter opener under his right index finger - the fingers are so white, freezer-burnt, knuckles like grape ice cream. Anyway, I got my scraping, fuck him. Weirdo.

Sunday

I stole my mom's pill dispenser. Seven little yellow plastic lids, one for each day of the week. I taped labels on them: "Paul's hair", "Fingernail & scraping", "Blood", "Semen", "Assorted Fibres", etc. I'm going to start the DNA test next weekend: so far blood type is a check. The fibres are a trick. Most of them are so common that they say nothing conclusive. I've spent hours separating them – they should really have their own dispenser. Up close, they all curl like question marks, same with the pubics. That level of inspection has always had a tendency to mock me. I gotta get the DNA test, a silent sea of ruin that always gives up its dead.

Monday

Paul took another run into the States tonight. There he was, hoppin' around, all excited, trying out some new Gangsta persona, and he's got this tiny tape recorder clenched in his fist. The whole ride, it's like I'm with two guys – one's Paul, the asshole, and the other one describes himself into his hand, and I guess there's a third, cause the description doesn't fit anybody I see. So, fuckface is keepin' up this rap about killin' bitches, fuckin' up hos, and I'm thinking this friendship is very fucking goofy. Anyway, I made my contact, got the software I need to start the DNA test. When I get back to the car, The Dork wants to know what I was doing. I had already thought of that. I hand him a cassette, some little girl-gang thing called "Floss #17." He asks, I tell him, "No, it's not a happy ending."

Tuesday

My semen sample is fucked. So I hid my van in Paul's Camaro (for future surveillance), and hung out inside Karla all day. Very uncomfortable. About eight inches of relatively smooth travelling, then it turns up into the body cavity. No fuckin' way I'm going up there for anybody, so I found a little interruption in the wall that I could hold on to. I squeezed so tight that my thumb met my fingers through the membrane. Once I settle, I realize that the place is all torn up, like shredded curtains. Networks of veins, exposed by ruptures, are turning and moving all around me. It looks like a belly lined with worms. Suddenly the whole place heaves forward and blows backward, and I'm almost thrown up into God knows what. Luckily I'm far enough back that I only get pressed against. Soon I have my sample. I'll get you fuckers yet.

You know, I'm lookin' at all the evidence I have – the DNA, the fibres, the copied tapes – and I'm thinking that the really damning recording has always been there: Karla Homolka. Not the woman, her name. Those five syllables covering both the perpetrator and her hapless victim; the site of the crime was given to her at birth and the crime is in the criminal's name. Typically. The tongue fits between bared teeth. What are they doing? Who are they doing it to? These are the questions I should have been asking all along. Soon everyone will be saying that name, tricked into taking part in these crimes. This is going to make them sick. Kar-La Ho-Mol-Ka. Holy Fuck, it was in the name all along.

Thursday

I had sex with you-know-who this morning. At least that's legal. If only for the last four years. He was sweet, he even kissed me goodbye and wished me good luck. I think he's figured out what I'm up to: it's impossible to keep secrets from the one you love. I'm getting twisted by this: when he came, I almost reached behind for a sample. I'm sorry, my darling, but I think this will change things between us forever.

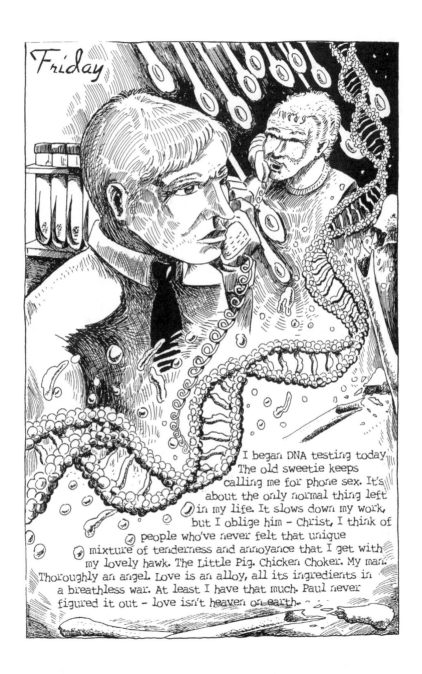

3. AT THE COURTHOUSE LAST JULY

Someone sold me a transcript of Cassette Tape Exhibit Numbers 352 and 353 for two dollars. You recorded this tape after Karla left for good. Alternately weeping and humming along to the soundtrack from *Free Willy*, you told her how much you loved her, and said you were going to kill yourself. Crying out, The Grim Reaper! Oh, ohhhhhh, he's here! This is it, ARGGHHH. At some point, you passed out in a drunken stupor: gowilly thassagoodwhale.

I stood outside the courthouse with a sheriff named Charles, whose black hair was combed in marcelled waves, who said don't be nervous. He told me that someone else was being transported in as we spoke, someone who looked just like you. I thought about the inevitable chains of simulations: a farmer in Pike Bay, Ontario, creating a mould of your face and growing cabbages, cauliflowers, in your image.

Then I headed up to courtroom 6:1 and stormed the place with a straight-razor hidden in my steel toed shoes that tripped the alarm (not the razor), the guards laughing and waving me inside. Once you were seated I grabbed the person closest to me and made a motion to slash his throat. I frog-walked him to the front to make the switch, approaching you with murder on my mind. Guns levelled at me, a gauntlet of black barrels. Let's do it, I said

I did not. I was the girl in the flowered shorts who cried all the time; the man who scratched at his neck until it bled; the teenage boy in a Grateful Dead shirt who borrowed paper from a journalist (me) "in case I want to take some notes."

I am a poet, Jean Genet writes in *Miracle of the Rose*, confronted by your crimes, constructing a poem from Exhibit Numbers 352 and 353.

November Rain (Cardinal Ideograms)
— P. J. Teale

A policeman. Polite.
Wearing visored cap.
— May Swenson

0   You're so beautiful; I let you down. I'm going to give you my soul
     and look right at you.

     I love you I love you I love you I love you I love you I love you.

     I used to tell people that in the morning the sunlight would come
     through the window

     the upstairs window shine
     down the corridor and highlight your face just
     illuminate it.

     I don't know if I ever told you that.

1   When I get to the other side I'm going to make it better for you.
     I'm going to set something up there real nice so when you come it
     will be alright.

     Less than zero, I tried to be larger than life.

2   I walk through the house sometimes and I go Kar Kar Karla Kar hey
     Kar but I don't get any answer.

     I fucking called for you so fucking much.

3   my heart's on fire I love you you little rat
    my little rat remember that my little rat
    the only person who ever loved me.

4   O God I hurt   O God I hurt
    in my tribulations in my violence
    through my confessions in my anguish
    in my pain in my joy in my sorrow.

5   please don't hate me
    please please please please please please
    don't hate me.

6   I really needed love in my life
    the four children I wanted.

    This is a lonely place
    my life's over: I want you to remember

    Some things are worth dying for.

7   I really wasn't that bad.
    You just don't understand.

    I'll go to jail for as long as I have to
    hope hope —

    There is hope in things, things
    or as we wanted to say it was till death do us part.

    I don't know how to stop.

8   In Hawaii it was
     beautiful in Hawaii.

4. The Drugs That Killed Tammy

Tammy sat on the front steps of her house staring at her sister's boyfriend while he scrubbed the tires of his car. A friend walked over from across the street. "How do you keep your hands off him?" she whispered...
— Nick Pron, *Lethal Marriage*

Paul started coming around in the fall. He would stand in our driveway shirtless, buffing his car, the sun picking out saffron streaks in his hair. He looked cut, tendons flexing, muscles in relief. The flat stones we tried to skim into the Niagara Gorge the night he kissed me.

I was thirteen years old, and I loved him. I think. My diary then was like an old song — *hey Paul, I want to marry you* — secured with a gold key I kept taped behind my headboard. I would squirm on his lap, asking him if I was prettier than Karla, wrestle him to the carpet until his breath was shallow. I loved Karla too, and was jealous of her.

Her hair dyed like a flowerbed, green and impatiens red. The music of her jewellery, anklets. Silver bracelets orbit her wrists and lilt when she walks, the Jupiter Symphony. Her girlish bedroom, silver-tasselled half-moon pillows, white lace skirts on bed and bureau. Where her makeup is: I slip in and rouge my lips and cheeks, try on her earrings (made from peacock feathers), her jet-black slip clasped at the breast and shoulders with roses.

I lie on her bed and close my eyes, touching the silken ears of her rabbits asleep beside me, listening to the hamsters and rats, turning on their wheels. Ariel, the cat, prowls the edge of the bed, murmuring — *in a cowslip's bell I lie*. There is a pair of handcuffs, looped over the bed-post: Karla always wanted to be a police officer, because she's smart and mean. I hear her return and I hurry from the room, erasing my traces from the coverlet, rubbing at the scarlet lines, her makeup's distemper.

Paul rubbed the white Capri with a chamois until it shined, and he offered me a ride. To cross the border and rest by the Falls, briefly. Holding me, he said I was the best thing in his life, that I was innocent and pure.

Touching me as though I would break. I had imagined this moment. To somehow be alone with him, with the windows rolled down, the stars rushing fast. That he would kiss me this way, once. Night and sleep devouring the rest.

I have watched the flesh fall from my bones lately, an analogue. As decay descends the pure white emerges: Paul's labour with the chamois; the unsteady movement of the handkerchief, soaked in halothane.

And I become confused. I used to dress and undress him in my head. Like a doll from my collection "The World of Love." I had thought of Adam this way, removing his tiny studded bellbottoms and velour shirt and placing him beside the girls: Flower, Soul, Peace, and Love. Chewing on his feet and folding him back into the purple carrying case (*where Love and her friends groove together*). In a nest of capes, suede fringes, psychedelic maxi-skirts, hangers, a heart-shaped umbrella the size of a parasol in a cold spiked drink (*One ice ice baby to go*, Paul said to me, the night I died). There is such distance in girls' dreaming: want, and what is withheld. In order to control yourself. How I used my doll boy's limbs, smooth head, and long, cool body: I turned him on between the girls, for them, and they were nasty.

Whipping him with their chainbelts and plastic handbags — Peace driving her pointed shoes into his chest while Soul raked him over with her afro-pick. Flower covering his face with her wide-brimmed hat and Love looking on, oblivious.

As I was, when Paul watched me through my curtains, believing in innocence the way that pirates did, explorers. Something simple: a ship off-course, an island seen through a spyglass. Grass skirts undulating, women breaking berries, letting the juice flow over their sienna skin, my long white hair. Longer still, as the skin shrinks from my skull. The vermin here have destroyed his letter to me. Placed on the quilted velvet inside my casket: *my life will never be the same now that you're gone*. A feast of *x*'s and *o*'s they attack like anoplura, sucking lice, and do not falter.

They will uncover me inch by inch.

The skeletonized body that rose to accuse him. I offered myself to this tenderness, the postmortem sweetness of combs, cotton, and light. They dispatched me very quickly.

Paul was fast and Karla felt ill. She thinks of me every day in prison as she makes her plans to leave. She knows she wants children, that she will colour her hair black.

Thinking of me, barely alive, I wonder, of the dark swarm of the night crawlers, denuding me.

5. By Any Other Name

We're changing our name, Karla wrote to a friend, to "Teale." Like the colour, she added, teal-blue. A darkish blue-green, suggesting plush draperies, bottle-glass, the tail of a five-lined skink, wedged underwater.

Phenomenologist Teale — names altered by a consciousness, an experience of something other. Paul is, clearly, an adequate name: *De ses yeux et de ses mains, il transforme le quotidien en merveilleux:*

> Gauguin Uccello Picasso Cézanne.

> Painters of seas and battles, bowls of fruit. Studies in light and form. Passion, by another name.

> Paul the Apostle to the Corinthians —

> The First Epistle:

For it is written, I will destroy the wisdom of the wise, and will bring to nothing the understanding of the prudent.

Kenneth Bernardo, however, will not do. Kenneth is your father's name, Bernardo as well. Son of Frank, a Portuguese immigrant labourer also known as The Tile Man, who laid squares of terrazzo and marble, who held you in his arms and blessed you, who closed his eyes to his child's proclivities. Kenneth, accountant and churchgoer (rapidly assessing the holdings of the collection plate, measuring growth, attrition), father, voyeur, sexual suspect.

His child inheriting many of these qualities, matriculating with relative ease, his strong arms inclined to work with concrete, power tools.

A love of little girls (I just want to talk to you, he said to me, pulling me into the apartment corridor and squeezing my thighs and I cried *I want to go home*). Did he touch you too, Paul? The psychiatrist I see, about this man and that, has suggested you experienced some blunt trauma in your childhood, because of your silence, your exile (hiding under the covers when you hear his light footsteps, his hand gingerly testing doorknobs, *I just want to talk*), and cunning. Let Kenneth become Jason; let Bernardo become Teale. And by alteration, change yourself. Teale (Thiel), the remorseless murderer of film whose secrets, he says, will be known some day. Jason, the star of *Friday the Thirteenth*, someone you could model yourself after, who could have been modelled after you.

6. JASON LIVES

Bernardo's counsel, Tony Bryant, informed the press yesterday that his client is not responding to his mail, or to any attempts to communicate with him...

You may still be wondering who I am. (*Who am I?* Bud Fox asks in *Wall Street*, as he stares at the Manhattan skyline from his penthouse apartment. He doesn't know what he's become, and now he's uneasy about Gekko's ideas: Pal, he tells him, the illusion has become real.)

Hey pal, hello Paul. The artist Ron Giii talks about illusion often. An eeluusion, is how he says it; he paints series of little carnival people, flying, walking tightropes. It's an opera, an alphabet, an attempt to point to something ineluctable, performative, about the way we go through our days.

(With the other masquerades/That time resumes)

I read, these lines from Eliot sometimes, for his sense of some *infinitely suffering thing* he can't imagine. I talk to people and tell them I am writing something fiendish. The next thing I write will be lovely, I tell them, a blazon. Pretty eyes and pink lips, alabaster — I mention you, and everyone starts to shift and frown, that horrible man. A MONSTROUS SEXUAL PREDATOR.

A friend described the arrest of a murderer today, in New York City. He was very attractive, he said, and added *if you're going to go that way, the guy may as well be good-looking.* I laughed at his gall, and was shocked. I can still be startled, which reassures me because I'm not nice, Pal.

I'm as mean as a snake.

Which is why I watch movies alone. I can't go to theatres. People make me angry, talking, yelling. Kill the bitch. And so on.

Alone, I have such illusions about art. The way my father would arrange three pears, just so, on a windowsill; my tiger cat on a tiger pillow; the tragic masque of Jason Voorhees.

The wilderness he inhabits, his longing for a taste of blood (in Candomblé, this refers to consanguinous desires, rooted in narrative).

At the moment, I am a student of psychoanalysis, writing you a serious letter, something personal, in order to gain your trust. This letter is real and I expect an answer (you are alone on the high wire, I am holding my breath: the suspense). It begins:

Dear Paul Bernardo,

I am currently preparing a paper which explores the implications of your attempt — in the early 1990s — to have your name legally changed. As a student of psychoanalysis, I find your case particularly intriguing. I am speaking specifically of your decision to borrow, nominally, from film.

I have examined similar relationships in my field research, and have published these findings in a number of small academic journals.

My own mother is germane to my research: she named me Elizabeth, having watched *Suddenly, Last Summer* the day I was born. She could not shake the way Taylor's eyes looked, as the urchins stormed the sea with their claws bared, consuming skin and bone. That they are violets, striped with black; that they may bloom in violence, tempests shaking the pine and cedar, *mutinous winds*.

An accident of circumstance, a left-handed way of offering me what she could not give me outright. Elizabeth, Queen — mistress of the wild with velvet spurs, wildcat in a half-slip, Nile Goddess, snake charmer.

I suggest that when you renamed yourself you were committing an act of patricide, and embedding, within yourself, another narrative, one which was more relevant to your self-perception. The title I have proposed for my paper is "Little Hands Clenched in Strangulation: Paul Bernardo and the Contemporary Horror Film."

Briefly stated, I intend to create an etiology, using incontrovertible hypotheses, regarding the connection between the *Friday the Thirteenth* sequence and your various sexual pathologies and perversions. I will examine your choice of the name "Jason" as one which reflects your affinity with this filmic character, citing the European origins of your surnames (Voorhees/Bernardo); your similar refusal to "die", or rest, under the nominal weight of your fathers' names; the incestuous impulses latent in your relationships with your mothers (signified by the tropes of Oedipal masking and maternal violence); and the locus of your violence, which, in its acceleration and repetition, indicates the constant restatement of (the first) crime, whereby the original pleasure principle continues to acquire different tensions and meaning.

I intend to refer to the mother-son paradigm that provides the films' central referent: the Anglo-Saxon epic *Beowulf* (*he struck so angrily that it bit her hard on the neck, broke the bone rings*); and I will gesture to the Romantics, whose affinities with both nature and the incest-model are well-documented.

Romantic that I am, I hope that you will write to me, because I need you. To prevail upon yourself, and offer me some confirmation, of the essence of my argument, the passion of my conviction, that my observations are of value, that I am

yours truly —

POSTCARD: PENCIL PUZZLES AND WORD GAMES

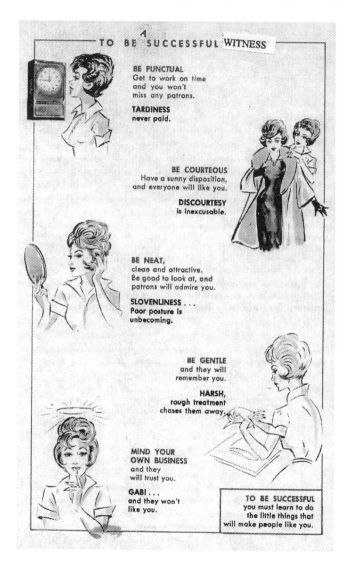

1. CHANGELINGS

Change the first word into the second word, one letter at a time.

A. Rape to Kill (4)

Rape Ripe Rile Rill Kill

2. CRYPTOGRAM

Decode the following sentence, in which series of letters is replaced by another (the words are spaced and ordered correctly). Example: Hit and Run, Pxy lqs Joq...

Kosv caqal zplhalah fyt loka qybwyzt; Nolvo toxt fa't o zplhalal.

3. WORD FUN

How many words/phrases can you make from the following sentence?

Here lies Paul and Karla.

Paul lies
rapes
kills
Karla lies

4. Movie-Mania!

On the left are the titles of four well-known movies that the Bernardos enjoyed. On the right are short descriptions of these movies. Can you match the titles with the descriptions?

1. *Wall Street*   a. Woman claims that a bad-ass makes her heart beat faster
2. *Friday the Thirteenth*   b. Lesbian psychopath goes on a killing spree
3. *Angel Heart*   c. Evil businessman is ratted out by his accomplice
4. *Deadly Innocents*   d. Masked psychopath is destroyed by a young woman

7. THE NIGHT OF THE IGUANA

How calmly does the orange branch
Observe the sky begin to blanch
— Tennessee Williams

Oh Paul, I mass love you. Paul Kenneth Bernardo is such a dude. I love you.
— Lori Homolka's inscription on the Bernardos' kitchen bulletin board

Even though he started giving me the creeps after Tammy died, I started to like Paul. Nights at the Bayview Drive house, drinking, while he smoked dope from a honey bottle. Exhaling a thin, blue stream and drawing it back in, chasing the dragon. I would look at his ice-blue eyes, his cowlick, and think, I love you. Right here, in this dollhouse, I love you like a bride. Which is what I meant when I said *Is jealousy a reason?* that these two should not be wed. As Karla's wedding skirts whispered when she turned to kiss him, when she lifted them to show her green lace garter.

I remember these pangs, and then I think of October, how cold I feel as this month arrives. That one night, that I return to: when what I felt collided with what I knew. As if the space between day and night was erased, and this changed me. Although I still love Karla, and wish she was here with me. Maybe we could talk about when, suddenly, you know something in you has died but you still go on, recalling —

Leaves, red and orange, held fast to the trees, some scattered like little hands in the grass. Moon-lights like fireflies in perimeter, the pale pink house. October — there are miniature pumpkins and gourds in bowls, the night hangs back like a ghost, star-pocked and black. Paul and his friends are getting high. I am aware of his presence, his warmth, a little burn where he kissed me hello. Karla and I are standing in the kitchen with Marlene. She is running her hands over Marlene's belly, feeling the baby stir and kick. She says it feels like rummaging underwater and bumping into fish. She asks if it is a girl, does it hurt when its fists pummel the wall. Marlene tells her it is like the kneading of bread dough when her baby decides to rise.

Marlene asks when Karla is going to have a child of her own. Paul calls into the room: She can't even leave the soap where I ask her to. In the dish. By the sink. She'd forget to feed and clean the baby and it would die.

I start to feel bad. I am thinking of babies, lying in their own filth, crying. I try to tease Karla but she is looking away. At the cabinets, as if they are filled with hidden bars of soap. Dove-curved into bassinets, ribboned, like christening gowns, with fine white shavings. But then she brightens, thinking of Spike.

When the iguana was brought into the clinic, he was dying. His owner never came back, and Karla took care of him. She washed his bright green body, scouring between the tooth and plate-shaped scales of his neck and head with a quilt square. She kept him near the sun, medicated him and tempted him with locusts and sunflower seeds. When he was better, she brought him home, naming him after his scale-crest, his pointed teeth.

Come see my baby, she says, and we go look at him in his terrarium, in his nest of wheatgrass and stones. He looks at us unblinking, his short tail twitching almost imperceptibly. My sweetheart, Karla says, pulling him out and cradling him. I reach over to pet him and he snaps at me, bites my finger. Marlene gets some gauze and disinfectant while I stand faintly over the kitchen sink, Karla saying I'm sorry I'm sorry.

Paul, Kevin, and Mark, now laughing by the terrarium. Paul sweet-talking someone named Stella and prodding the iguana, baiting her, baiting him. I watch from the doorway as he smacks the glass and lowers his hand. The spiny tail whips and cuts him. He squeezes the tail, hard, and is bitten as well. Furious, he is yelling and I am backing away. He rinses his hand in the sink and rages; he storms away. I look fearfully at the droplets of blood tracked along the counter, the marks in my hand. Like a vampire's kiss. The floor seems to sway and I fall, and rise.

Paul returns to the kitchen with Spike. I'm going to kill you, he screams, and I am elbowed aside. Karla's arms are raised and I stand still as he slams the iguana on the carving board and beats it with the blade of a knife. It's twitching and striking its tail and Paul slams the knife over and over into its neck, slicing its head off while its legs knead the air and blood flows and pools in the wooden grooves. He comes over to Karla and touches her shoulder, leaves a red leaf there.

Calm down, he tells her, ignoring me, although I am trembling. When he passes me, I feel a different tremor. Blunt and frigid, icicles plunging from lips of glass and piercing the lesser heat, of snow.

Clean it up and skin it, he says. Try not to tear it. Cool and smiling now, she dissects it with an X-Acto knife, explaining the procedure. She makes an incision in his neck and slices down, pulling the flesh aside in two wings, which reminds me of those awful paintings of Christ revealing his sacred heart. Karla points out his lungs and testicles to Marlene, as she unpeels the skin from his clawed feet and hands.

She looked so happy, arranging his organs into a diagram. Paul smiling too, making a puppet, his hand draped in scales of lime.

Cut it loose, I thought, as the rain began and Karla absently stroked the motionless tail, an act of absolution. I heard the mesquite chips shake onto the gas grill, and smelled smoke. Paul basted the iguana with wine and rosemary and turned it over with a fork. Black bars formed on its breast. Mark took a bite and said "delicious."

As Karla wrapped her arms around Marlene's waist, her face pinkened by the quickening flashes of light, I thought of God's creature at the end of its rope, and looked across the lawn — remembering:

> O Courage, could you not as well
> Select a second place to dwell,
> Not only in that golden tree
> But in the frightened heart of me?

Reciting this to myself, I turned back. I watched Paul devour every last bite, and still I stayed.

8. PORNOGRAPHY

MAN OF MY DREAMS

IF IT'S NASTY, SEND IT IN AND TURN OUR READERS ON!

Dear Lusty Letters,

I work at a maximum-security prison in Canada. The work is pretty routine, but being a female guard can be tough. I'm a horny early-thirties gal, and being so close to all that chained heat is enough to drive me crazy sometimes.

I spend a lot of time during my breaks frigging off after escorting some of these buffed and sex-starved specimens to the showers. I watch them, naturally, oozing into my panties as they soap their cock-shafts and piss-slits, their big hairy balls. I practically drool imagining all the cum they could shoot, but I'm all business when I'm with them (although I sometimes let them get a load of my full, milky tits when I bend down with the leg-irons).

I wanted to tell you about this one experience I had with a guy in segregation. He's pretty notorious, and I recognized him immediately. I'd always wondered if I would. Paul's locked up most of the time, so I figured his dick must be aching to fire off, and I wanted to be the one to see each creamy spasm.

I managed to bribe the two guards who monitor his cell: a couple of juicy blow jobs promised me easy access, and both guys promised to watch and get their rocks off again.

Paul is kind of shy and nervous, so when I snuck into his cell the other night, he looked a little wary. But when I stripped down to my red crotchless panties and fuck-me shoes, he popped a boner I thought would rip his prison greys in half.

I DID A SLOW, SEXY DANCE, LETTING HIM GET OFF ON MY HARD NIPPLES AND TIGHT GRINDING ASS.

By then he was about to shoot, even though I hadn't touched him yet!

Come here, you little girl-killer, I said. Let me give you what you need. He stumbled over on his knees, his uncircumscised prick glistening with pre-cum, his eyes glazed with lust. He asked me to bend over and I told him I was calling the shots. Bend over yourself, I said. You don't want to get on my bad side.

He lay against the cot and spread his ass cheeks while I put on some of my favourite spiked rings. I ran my hand over my dripping gash and rammed my fist up his ass while ripping at his foreskin with my long fingernails. Meanwhile, I was straddling his legs and cumming like crazy as he bucked against me, his face buried in the pillows.

My clit was still throbbing so I squatted on his back, grinding my heels into his spine and letting my juices stream over his throbbing hole. I frigged myself with the noose I had tied around his neck so I didn't have to see his fucking face, and screamed as I was rocked with another high-speed climax. When I was done I relieved myself — gave him a long golden shower and signalled to be let out. I was a little disappointed he didn't cum, since I thought he was into kinky loving. But after watching the tape again, while having my clit licked by my two associates, I realized I had found the man of my dreams.

My husband can never know, but I'm not going to let Paul get away from me this time.

— Lynette, Kingston

9. THE SCARBOROUGH RAPIST

ONE. JANE DOE # 13

I was walking home and I was afraid. I knew he was still out there. Angry because everything is menacing: elevators, alleyways, parking lots, woods, bus stops, my own house. I sleep with mace under my pillow, knowing that it's not enough: he will take it from me. Walking through life like a Marine, listening for the tell-tale sounds. A rustle of branches, leaves snapping, windows breaking, a baby-doll-trap at half-tide.

It could be anyone, there is no one I can trust. I live in his shadow always and I hate him for it.

When my mother died I walked away from the church in my only black dress, remembering how she hated me to walk alone — she followed me sometimes, ducking behind trees. You look good in black, he said, and I was ashamed.

He whistled and cat-called the day I ran through the park, my daughter unloosening from the jungle-gym, in mid-fall. Her arms outstretched, my starling.

I am in the emergency room looking down at my unbuttoned shirt, bloodied and remorseful.

My daughter's friends are ballerinas. She brought home patterns, for a net skirt and leotard. And cried when I burned them. Enrolling her the next morning in Tae-Kwon-Do, the cruellest of the martial arts. It's good, I told her, to possess grace.

I need to know that you can disable someone with your bare hands. That is graceful.

When you are thirteen I will buy you a gun. And we will fire at tin cans on the fence by the lake — artichokes — until you find the heart.

The Sisters dressed me in kilts and knee-highs, measuring the hem each day. Unconscious of how erotic this outfit is: "Fuck me in my uniform." I saw this in a sex advertisement. A girl with her legs spread, green and black plaid bunched up to show her white panties.

Thinking of the Kristen French testimony, thinking of men in the court-room looking at their laps. Caught — the means without end. I was there every day.

I sneak up on my daughter in the kitchen and she spins, she grabs me in a stranglehold and her tiger's eyes flash.

The mother cat we adopted, who taught her kittens to kill. We watched them follow her, learning to listen. To crouch, and pounce. We saw flocks of birds disappear. Before losing them, she gave them this.

I was walking home along Centennial Road, trying to stay in the light. He asked me what I was doing, and I walked faster. He grabbed me and threw me down, on the grass lot near where I live. Pinning my arms and sitting on my back; I tasted pesticides, weeds. You bitch. Whore. I'll kill you if you look at me, he said. Hitting my face and strangling me with rope, ripping off my skirt and raping me, asking me my name.

Betty, I said. Yes. Yes, I love you. He sighed soon and stood, emptying my purse and taking my wallet before kicking me in the ribs.

I lay there a long time after he had left, abrading my face against the teeth of the dandelions, listening, for the whisper of the night crawlers.

Later, the police administered the rape kit, taking anal and oral swabs, scanning my body with a Wood's lamp, its fluorescent light finding tracks of seminal fluid. I told them everything. What he looked like, what he wore. The way the streetlights hit the red stone of his Masonic ring.

I know nothing about Masons. Only that they are all men. That they use a secret handshake and meet in temples. Maybe the handshake is a blow to the head, I suggested. The rape crisis counsellor shook her head, and looked at the detective.

In some secret language of their own.

He just went on, attacking with impunity. Here's a little sample of my blood, Officer.

Misplaced — like all of his mementos. The rope and dagger; the locks of hair; the scraps of dresses. The picture of my daughter he took from me. She is older now, almost fourteen. He wouldn't recognize her.

Should she walk past his cell at night, whistling low, crouching. Handgun like a second skin, safety never caught. But released, again and again she goes down to the water, and stands there. Her adamant arms entwined in arabesque.

TWO. THE MIDNIGHT RAMBLER: PAUL'S CONFESSION
I M CALLED A HIT-AND-RUN RAPER, IN ANGER

You got no confession, you got no case
— Paul Bernardo

Bernardo frequently (late in the evening) recorded his rap ideas, music, and lyrics so he wouldn't forget them. In all, police took 1,000 sheets of song lyrics from 57 Bayview Drive, 105 of them original Bernardo words. Trial judge Patrick Le Sage ruled the prejudice the tape and lyrics would cause would far outweigh any relevance and ruled them inadmissible...
— The Toronto Sun, *September 1, 1995*

The poem then...is essentially about an imaginary character (not the poet, not me) named Henry...
— John Berryman, Note, *The Dream Songs*

The whole point is that I'm going into my mind &
showing how much I   Enjoy   my reckless fucking life.
I am the sôlo creep I make the girls weep   *and she is chilly*
acting out my crimes, while the others sleep.   *& lost*

I stalk'd like the wolf and you were my prey —
Just leave me with the things I want, that please me,
cause it feels so right, as I fade into the night *mer*   *stupid questions*
so come with me,   Don't   ask me where   *asked me*
(I don't know.)   *move me to homicide —*

I've got no rémorse & I've got no shame.
Did you ever get caught. No, never. Why?
Because I'm a *deadly* innocent guy.
The illusion has become real, how does it Feel?   *I'll take an ax*
I'm the big wheel, Paul Jason Teale.   *to her inability*

THREE. BERNARDO REMEMBERS THE SCARBOROUGH RAPES:

10. TALES FROM THE CRYPT

Which we all like. Rain. When we sleep. But wait until our sleeping. Drain.
— James Joyce, Finnegan's Wake

Theres one story about a house in Port Dalhousie thats been torn to the ground now theres just a space cryptlooking and ghastly where it was sweetcoloured pink and palest white faraway theres a man who sits in a jail at night O terrifying with the fierce dogs prowling the perimeter hes crumpled in fear his nightshirt and pillow drenched with sweat pissyellow his eyes are widestaring Im sure the way Hamlets were when he saw the pale figure of the king the very same as the bars slide open hes harrowed with fear and wonder and the girls come in all dreadful dressed in wet leaves and dirt leaving a trail of water a tributary and one is bald another in pieces the thirds face all burned their eyesockets empty but theres vermin like worms and small spiderish bugs web their bony fingers reaching theyre falling on him and hes screaming tragic sounds hes sorry hes sorry theyre pulling him apart and its a whirl except his mouth open a black O the last panels this guard Im remembering he sees an empty bed and one weed dropped by the bars a fern I think green and delicate hes fearstruck theyve left a picture in their place its drawn in blood and hes staring up his keys fallen clink clink its these plumred angels rising high over this empty space where theres a burial mound like a dogs but staked with crossed spikes one theyve left white and with moistened hands made the other a faint belladonna pink.

11. MAHAFFY

1. LESLIE'S NOTEBOOK

Friday — late

I'm writing this outside of Mac's Milk. I just ripped off this cool thing for Ryan — candy that comes in a pink plastic brain. Called Amanda and I can't come over, it's too late to wake up her mom, I told her all about Martin walking me home and who else stayed at the Rock. How we were listening to "Forever Young" like a hundred times and I was thinking about Chris and really feeling bad. Thinking about him just cruising and not even knowing and Smack it's all over. Liz said that he was all crushed up and his face was covered in glass like he was crying. I wrote I Will Love You Always on a tree with Kelly's knife. We were all drinking beer, and Mike was passing around that purple grass he calls Barney. A bunch of us were holding hands and saying Chris wouldn't want us to be sad and the song was playing and I thought he'll stay young and we won't, like I wouldn't know him anymore and I felt worse. It's weird because I didn't feel anything at the funeral home, everything was so unreal, all that velvet and the smell of flowers like Glade. That undertaker's cold hands, the way he made Chris up to look so pure. It was really fake but kind of beautiful. I was remembering the time I was wasted and thought I was dying and all the stones I saw were little caskets and I went home and looked at Ryan, just looked at him all night. His face buried in the blankets and the slow sweet way he breathed. It helped me breathe. Even though Mom was yelling at me in the morning because she could tell by the way I looked I had a massive hangover. I know they're both really mad at me now and I'm screwed because I reek of dope and it's really late. I wish I still had my key. William called me a social butterfly tonight when I was drinking and just flying around and dancing when The Doors were on, when he goes I'll never look into your eyes — Again, it's like he's right inside me. Oh yeah, the cops came and busted us after the fire we made got into the trees. It was amazing because they all looked like devils in the red light, just burning. So Martin As I Was Saying walked me home and we stopped and he kissed me about three times and he grabbed my hand and played with my mood ring. When it turned red he went Oh you must like me. I was trying to hide my braces and he said they were cool, like a train-set, which was cute (I think) and he said I should wear white more since I'm blonde and he walked me all the way to my house and we tried the side-door and windows but they were locked. I said it was okay, I'd go in the front, and he left. I tried the front door and it was locked too and that's why I'm here.

It's later and I'm sitting in the backyard and I don't know what to do. If I ring the bell I'll be in serious trouble. There's some guy walking around in a hooded shirt, he looks like a burglar but he's nice. He said I should throw a rock at the window and I said no way. I'm going to go ask him for a cigarette and then I'll just sleep under the picnic table and sneak inside in the morning. I'm scared. I can see my bedroom from here and I'm so tired. Please don't be mad at me Mom, Dad. It's creepy here but peaceful too. I hear crickets and I bet you're waiting up for me. Don't lock me out, don't —

let me go I want to see my family I just want to see Ryan please let me go

2. Debbie

The mother may sometimes suffer the child to fall and to be distressed in various ways, for its own benefit, but she can never suffer any kind of peril to come to her child, because of her love.
— Julian of Norwich

Near the shore the top twelve inches of water were permanently packed with transparent fish smaller than sardines, the young of a species we have not identified. We called them "Plexiglas fish." For a diver they created zero visibility near shore.
— Jacques Cousteau, *The Living Sea*

I received the news alone: ovarian cancer, and my chances of conceiving slim to none. My husband came home and during this time, imagined our baby for me. Reciting the names of oceanographic vessels, one by one

L'Hirondelle, the Challenger, the Talisman. Remembered ships that battered the waves, discovering life under water:

Shark Whale Manta Ray, his hand makes a little octopus, crawls across my eyes and I dream, seeing her in sonar, swimming among the plankton, the siphonophores, the white medusas.

My body breaks to deliver her. I watch her struggle to breathe, and she rests, locked in my arms. A red sea flower,

blind spindrift, her hands and feet pearled. Sapphire eyes with beaded lashes, her milky body curling in languid strokes.

I refuse these thoughts. The smell of her hair, the blue blanket she guarded nervously, the sound of her small steps, following me. Blissful anguish,

narcotics preceding surgery. I am sick with worry, if she is late if it rains if she turns away from me: she wanted me to leave her alone, always alight with pleasure.

Pain, its corollary. I don't understand

death, she cried that day, plaintively. She wore pale silk and lilies she would
unhand to the casket, unfettered, her coral necklace without its key.

I love you she said, I said I love you,
my daughter, sinking in blacked-out coffins, beneath the sea.

Yet close enough to call to me (as a girl she had terrors):
Have I died? Her odd fears, the horror of my sins, not loving her wisely
too well do I feel her tremors, the current of her tears.

As she looks at the latched window beyond the moon's garish glow, a
woman offers her a bear to hold if she is frightened:

how Kind you are I said.

Instead she falls trembling. The door pushes inward, in minutes her heart
ends and begins

before she is strangled again and broken. That is not my daughter, those are
not her eyes: brown stones, a barrier

reef where the mermaid kicks and tumbles beneath my hands. She resides in
the Temple of the Sea, and defying him, she comes to me:

I am asleep and she comes to me alone
Screaming

I turn and see it is over,
Leslie is still not coming home.

— Dan Mahaffy, August 31, 1995

3. DAN

When Debbie was ready to come home with Leslie, I brought them flowers. One long-stemmed yellow rose, and a baby's breath corsage I pinned to the layette.

The night I crashed my car I thought of them, waiting for me. My ribs crushed and forehead lacerated, the windshield shattered, florescent white.

In the hospital I learned origami. Leslie was too young to visit. I sent her paper baskets filled with folded flowers.

She began to write things I didn't understand. Sad poems. There was one about a girl who was shot to death up north. "Her hair crowned with field daisies", she wrote, and I cried. I don't think she saw me.

We were not as close then. I remembered bringing her to the Botanical Gardens. Watching her run through the pathways, *the sunflowers are lifting their faces*.

I did bring her chrysanthemums on Valentine's Day. She kept them on her dresser. Her door was usually locked.

Her newborn face was a crumpled flower.

Fine yellow hair, her face lifted to the sun.

The summer day we buried her I noticed the ground was choked with blooms. All over our house, in wreaths, foil-wrapped pots, and bunches. The air was thick with their sweetness.

I ripped them all apart. I sat on the floor twisting and breaking them.

Watching the pollen spread over all the whiteness, her baby's dress of lace and linen, the rosebud nestled there.

12. THE GREEN KNIGHT

Green is the colour of my avarice, wanting all of you — and the envy of those who have turned away, not wanting to fight with monsters, because they may become monsters themselves.

I am an amorphous green monster. Raging through a tiny hamlet, stamping on cars and pedestrians, lifting the roof of your jail. One flat reptilian eye, fixed on you.

I am lying on my couch like Camille, with a sick headache, covered in a pea-green blanket and reading fourteenth-century poetry. The anonymous poet who wrote *Pearl*, and *Sir Gawain and the Green Knight*.

Pearl is an elegy, where terrible loss is mitigated by faith: the speaker's dead daughter transcends her grave, and reaches a heaven that is indescribable to you.

The structure of elegy has consoled me; I am studying Firearms Repair, and I need to know that what is broken can be fixed.

Sir Gawain is also a religious poem (I woke today hearing voices, a gospel choir singing: *Help me in my weakness, for I'm falling out of grace*).

Jesus   this sort of thing troubles me.

As though something within you knows better: green was my favourite colour as a child because I felt sorry for it. No one ever picked it and I thought, looking around me, that it deserved better.

Green leaves of grass, greensleeves.

My thoughts return, as rhymes dictate they must, to the beginning. When I saw you that summer's day, a cultivated monster, in green.

The poem begins in Camelot, on New Year's Day. A huge green knight arrives at Arthur's feast, shimmering in opulent gemstones.

Olive eyes, lush leaves pressed in armour, sweetgrass hair and silk raiment.

He berates the men of the Round Table from his celadon steed; his red eyes and sage spurs flash as he challenges them: May the wildest of you strike me, and allow me to return the stroke.

One stroke for another, he offers, laughing at the terror of these legendary knights.

Sir Gawain offers his loyalty, heart, and life, receives the King's blessing, and approaches the Green Knight. His axe shining as it falls, cleaving the head at its start.

He watches with disbelief as the Green Knight stands, holds his head between lichen hands.

And speaks: To the Green Chapel you will go, and on the first day of the next new year, be dealt the same blow.

Gawain departs after All Hallow's Day; he travels through cruel woods until he prays for Christ's assistance.

He makes the sign of the cross three times and is transported to a great Lord's castle paradise.

There, the Lady comes to him for three nights, opening his bed-curtains, revealing her headdress of pearls, and faultless face

(of heavenly climes).

She offers him her bright green kirtle, silk with golden bands, so that he may be protected from the hand of the green knight, from any sublunary craft.

Gawain arrays himself in his red vestments on the morning of the new year, winds the kirtle, serpentine, without. And offers his head to the verdant knight, who strikes him three times, leaving but one tender scratch. The green knight was the Lord, bewitched by sorcery; the Lady matched him in fidelity, she offered Gawain the three kisses at the Lord's behest.

To demonstrate the order of his allegiance, her own devotion, matchless and blessed.

The Lord speaks: *In you is villainy and vice, and virtue laid low.*
Gawain replies: *Your cut has taught me cowardice, care for my life.*

And the inspirited knight retreats from the castle ornamented. With spires of gold that rise in eminence to meet the hallowed skies.

He returns and speaks with shame and fury to his court. Mortified at what he must show: the scar that collars his neck, viridescent, moss-grown.

The poem's meaning is clear: in a world where you can replace your own severed head, you do not need to be protected.

That faith is when you stop asking questions.

You are so quiet, it makes me wonder. If you are asking that your broken soul be blessed. Or if you are too busy, rinsing your food in the sink, lost in introspection.

Knowing you are smaller than life, that you must shape your memories until they are stacked in neat, folded piles. One in particular, the green garter that Karla wore under her wedding dress, lost in the ceremony.

Waking and refusing exercise, unfolding each memory with a shake. As though some currency will slip out, from the white envelopes you opened on your honeymoon, making a carapace of green: grass-lots; your mistress's eyes; squares of plaid; the skin of the iguana.

The colour of your one good suit. You bought it when you were an aspiring accountant. Confident you would spend many years, staining your faithless fingers, that everything you touched would be as emerald, rare and coveted, assailable. Your eyes closing tonight, your thoughts wander, in fields of peerless green.

POSTCARD: MASH NOTES

He MADE me write him pillow notes like the chocolates in hotels he liked
and I HATED it I did hate this and you are a LIAR I used stickers yes SO?
He said I'd better watch my back and carried a KNIFE don't you get it can I
have some water That is my writing it is all a LIE

Honey,

If you go to Honouma
Bay and count each
polyp of coral in the
sea and all the
spines of the sea
urchins in the bay
and multiply that
number by infinity
that is how much I
love you

Your wife and best friend
Karla

Paul,

I'm chasing you and I'm
coming really close and I'm
gonna get you!

Love you

a good deal of the incidental symbolism
appears in these pillow notes
palm trees
stars   worms
dogs

LIPS:

a baby & two lions.

On pink and blue paper, cut into hearts,

Libretto, *Andrea Chénier* —

    A poet speaks of fields of violet, the sun crowning the firmament, of love.
You do not know what love is, he tells his aristocratic paramour. She weeps
for forgiveness, and Andrea orders, KILL THE POET. His lover is executed
with him,

A tragedy, the poems were written to excite to incite   Revolution,

a princess meets an artist and they are aflame. With discovery, deception,
and destiny,

LIES (Brava, I call, and clap and clap until my diva steps away from the stage).

13. Sex Trial

During the trial, Paul would occasionally draw figures on a legal pad:

He also wrote notes, which he would pass to his attorney:

Liar — She's fucking lying.
Ask her about SEX.
~~Where~~ How does she get off?

13.1 THE GHOST-TANTRIC ORGASM

The concurrence of sadism and masochism is fundamentally one of analogy only; their processes and their formations are entirely different; their common organ, their "eye," squints and should therefore make us suspicious.
— Gilles Deleuze

Maybe we could just talk about one or two things, and you could take your time. About sex for instance. Or language: interstice gap rupture lacuna. Unknown regions of discourse — when lips part to reveal recessed slits; where visibility is lost. The fricative sounds of your pleasure, an air current producing sound across a narrow, labial opening.

Even as you disappear. And emerge to reveal the seminal evidence — the cum-shot that is integral to pornography; specular, real. Undone at your sex trial by your own mechanism. The camera that cannot capture the concomitant embryological relic, the contractions and diminutive swelling that attend the female orgasm.

The climax that clenches, holding you tight, something powerful and frightening (a part of you is missing, captive). Something atomic, particular strength orbiting in unseen space; something that could destroy anything in its path.

Karla is *seen* receiving oral sex on many occasions. She says, under oath, that she did not enjoy it. There is no further discussion. Hesitant fingers turning her on, her own tongue extended in anticipation, end of discussion.

When journalist Nick Pron has the audacity to suggest that Kristen French may have been aroused during cunnilingus, his book is seized from libraries. A different press ban, as though sexual pleasure cannot be autonomous. Our Bodies Ourselves —

The binding contract in discussions of female sexuality, between body and mind. Significant and valuable, crossing guards at the points of entry, exit.

Erroneous also, as friction is pleasure. (Some victims speak of feeling shame about arousal, what is ignited when desire and hatred are split apart).

This contract offers Homolka the well-documented and political option to deny her participation in the rapes, all visual evidence to the contrary

(Christian...that...really...feels...nice).

13.2.

You will have a much greater understanding when you hear my testimony at the trial I promise you.

In the meantime, something that may help you is a wonderful book that I can't find any fault with — The Battered Woman *by Lenore Walker.*

Love, Karla

— Letter to Wendy Lutczyn

When Karla was awaiting her trial, and later, preparing her testimony for Bernardo's trial, she studied feminist theory and sociology, taking notes. (Like a trial-lawyer, she sought precedents, loopholes, legal context.) Catalogued on index cards, cross-referenced and arranged alphabetically, according to author and subject.

They Make Us Paint Our Face + Dance: Lennon, John. ★ Daly, M.: False Self boxed in coffins, re/hearsed & reversed ★ Woman as Vessel, See Dworkin, A. (Also Women as Chattel, sex + reproductive Slaves) ★ Lovelace, Linda: Away from captor, among people who have not suffered Terror as she + I have. Being Owned and Being Fucked. ★ Feelings of Helplessness, Isolation, Denying Terror and Anger, See Walker, Lenore E. ★ Low Self-Esteem, Lying as Survival: Walker. ★ Cooking and Cleaning Always, See: Morgan, Robin. ★ McKinnon, C.: Rape and Consent. ★ Greer, Germaine: Hair as secondary sexual characteristic. ★ Sisters in Crime/Hood is Powerful. Acting Out. ★ De Beauvoir, Simone: Cinderella-Myth. ★ Denial, Grief: Walker. ★ Cole, Susan: NOW, July 13-19, 1995: I am a Victim too ★ Destruction, Thrill-Seeking Females in Solanis, Valerie. ★ Immunity, Repressed Memories, Women Who Love Too Much. ★ Pillow Notes: The History of the Pillow Book, Women's Secret Rage. ★ Lovely You in Blue Hawaii, Presley, Elvis, Pathology of.

Shuffling her cards like a black jack dealer, fanning them on the stand. Ace showing, Queen face down, contrite.

13.3. WHIPLASH GIRLCHILD IN THE DARK

Wanda Van Sacher-Masoch objected to her own characterization in Leopold's *Venus in Furs*. Her husband, she claimed, had an exceedingly dominating personality; his masochism, as expressed in the novel, is more telling of the act of sexual, as opposed to actual, powerlessness.

Leopold chose to assume the masochistic position in sex, a position that is bartered among practitioners of S/M. Quite often it is the sexual "bottom" who is, in life, overbearing and powerful. (The "top," conversely, is often passive, lacking force and conviction in his/her day-to-day existence).

Paul, I'm asking you to think, is all. About wanting to be called The King in bed. How Houlahan nailed you on this point. That you were the dominant personality, that Karla's submission was evidence of her ongoing victimization.

About Karla screaming at you for using her crystal glasses, about your meek apology. And her description of your inferior intelligence; her impatience, initiative, aggression, tenacity, and rapier mind.

Of yourself cringing and weeping into a tape recorder while she was mailing topless photographs of herself to a new lover.

The theatre of S/M, a play in which fantastic parts are performed.

Since sex was erased from the trial (evanescing into the breach, of contract), you could not argue that if Baby, you're the bottom, she's the top.

14. The Journalist & the Murderer

...it was also clear that The King was one of those cruel rulers, only deigning to touch her when it was absolutely necessary for his own pleasure, never looking at her pretty face and many times hiding it...
— Christie Blatchford, "Bizarre Horror of the Ordinary." *The Toronto Sun*, June 2, 1995

Ms. Blatchford, who is writing a book on the case for Key Porter Books, is the journalist Paul hates the most.
— *The Globe and Mail*, December 4, 1993

It's strange to have something in common with you besides our age and horoscope sign. A Virgo born in the year of the Dragon, you are distinguished by your compulsive neatness and serene countenance.

And while it is true that a few of your schemes are just a little too far-flung and that you do a lot of things on the spur of the moment, you always manage to land on your feet.
— Oriental Horoscope, 1996, The Year of the Rat

I saw Christie Blatchford at the courthouse with several acolytes, young men, forming a protective circle. I have never spoken with her, and she may be a creature of charity (she was, after all, given a locket at the trial by an elderly woman who thanked her for her humanity).

And I followed her coverage of your trial, which was venemous. Her columns like sonnets, presenting ideas and deforming or restating them with an acidic *envoi*. About carving you a new asshole; about the cold beauty of the law.

She struggles with frigid adjectives, her love for the boys of winter (Gilmour breaks away, he fakes a pass — he scores!) informs her climatic prose.

Her work has always offended me: the way she carves blue lines through ideas, making equal and distant parts; the spaghetti western, her locus.

Yet, almost in spite of herself, her observations were embedded with something else. Humidity, the insidious heat of that awful summer. Even at night, the sun left its mark, imprinting sheer dresses, bare legs with a sheen, a viscous discomfort.

She wondered in print which hand you used to masturbate (*do you touch yourself in a sinister way?*); described your odd duskiness, grace, and almost girlish beauty.

Your pursed lips and jailhouse pallor; the way you thrust your hips, in unconscious recollection.

(Your pretty bow-mouth, as kissed by Cupid)

These comments beneath her outrage, like the impression of handwriting, left, barely visible, on the blank page below:

Christie loves Paul .

I used to watch a television show in the 1970s called Get Christie Love. Everything but the title has escaped me.

Which is what I had in mind when I read her column headed "Icy Bernardo Chills Soul."

I wonder if she's trying to reach you. To write your blue eyes as arctic, where no palm trees sway. Where there is no warmth (the fluent waves that creep beneath your bathing skirt and break).

To write herself, serious Christie. Who loves the law for its binaries, whose notions of beauty are almost poignant. Strange ducklings navigating the water, arching their necks and becoming swans; a caterpillar tearing at its chrysalis and taking flight in the colours of the Monarch; a desirable man she kills in her imagination each night. When she sees herself in the impenetrable monitor, and moves her fingers in exiguous fugues, remembering you.

15. Pretty Thoughts

(Paul dreams) he develops syphilis-dementia in prison, collects his "pretty thoughts" in jars:

is what the jars originally held though I have polished them now for seven hours sisters and stars and they are purple and green like bruises & the tulips wilted a little in the water but opening up like they are opening one two three four thighs for me to come and burst the flowers I grew with bulbs boxed in the basement in cells I have split cells it is not right to think of the blood and myself not eating for some time only petals in water beautiful but tasteless De Maupassant Why my necklace was paste! Not diamonds he became ill and all the Pretty charming girls in silk and furs were wraiths he tried to capture I am lining up the lids their metal bands shining and clasps to stopper these thoughts that have come loose and gather in the air like butterflies the black and gold of all the sweetness all the kilted legs and blazercrests her face in the sunlight how illuminated my vision of loveliness diamond window pane a woman undressing one breast bared to me then chiffoned its powdery weight the heft of keys and money in my pockets my hands there dishabille wrinkled where the green notes play a symphony the dough white texture of her in pieces I remember her a blazon head torso arms & that I could not eat not at all and the mint growing wild in the woods and winsome the wet earth where I sang the worms and their smooth bodies entwined my finger a ring with a red stone precious intoxicating (Jewels) the necklace on her throat I ripped away leaving a mark I left a mark on them my hand smothering them in the grass red stone raised catches moonlight Oh I love you an opera I lived for love soprano wings spread my pretty thoughts are high & pure escaping me there are crenulations in the brain rippling a stream jumping fish I saw silvery and I collect them slippery as blood I disdain as hot and screw the lids shut I see them shifting a prism they are hoarded between the towels I am clean immaculate are my preserves

16. THREE KILLERS

This is the face of a killer, isn't it?
— Ray Houlahan

Hey killer, you like that name, killer?
— Guard, to Paul Bernardo. Metro East Detention Centre, 1993

L ewis, Jerry Lee, nicknamed Killer, plays and burns his piano like the devil. Nights as a child peering through juke-joint windows and honky-tonks, rolling the keys like the Mississippi. Marries his 13-year-old blonde cousin and gets run out of town on a rail. Likes drinking wine spo-dee-o-dee; The Killer Rocks On. Baby-Snatcher; Chicken Hawk (Now let's git real low one time).

G ilmour, Doug, former centre for the Toronto Maple Leafs, number 93. Called the Killer, team captain, plays by the rules, plays to win. Stares at opponents with actual hatred, eyes vacant and dead. A shark, a Flame. Played for St. Louis in the mid-80s: rumours of   begin to circulate; traded to Calgary. Now a Devil, married to Amy, a young blonde, is a Milkman (I said shake, baby, shake).

B ernardo, Paul. Convicted murderer and rapist. Killed three girls, all under sixteen. Grandson of a marble-worker (St. Louis, the Patron Saint of), musician, formerly married to young blonde veterinary assistant. Likes tropical drinks and reefer, played road and ice hockey as a teenager. Pretty Boy, Night Crawler (Come on over, baby, baby you can't go wrong).

POSTCARD: OZARK

PAUL AND KARLA VISIT A PROSTITUTE, 1992

Now don't go drivin' off's what I said, I'll miss you like crazy. Talkin' trash, you know and ain't nobody gonna tell me I knew what them two was up to. My work's my own business and they was just customers. Clients is all, that blond bastard and his wife kinda sneerin' at me. It was Atlantic City. Summer. I was callin' myself Ivana cause of the Trump Plaza which is where they was stayin' at. Hits three hundred I told him, and I sat on her lap, cat-like, while he drove. When she and me was strippin' I noticed she had all kinds of bruises on her. I said, Damn, you look like a workin' girl. She said she had a big ol' dog named Buddy, forever hurtin' her. So I got her off and it coulda been nice n' easy cept Blondie's yellin' out directions, like suck on her titties! Until I says why don't y'all hire a maid? Then he tried to shove up my rear and I told him the Good Lord didn't make that for dicks. So he shoved up on me and started screwin', just on and on. I had to ask him to stop, my pussy just weren't built for him. He said I was a little on the aggres-sive side, started cryin' and beggin' for me to tell him I loved him. And I did, hits a fact, to get him off me and he never did come. I finally said I'm gone, y'all expect too much, and he sets to braggin' on how hard he always is, and I told him, you get yourself some help boy. Oh, and when I was in the ladies' he comes to the door and asks can he watch me. I got the hell away from them fuckin' weirdos I tell you, the shock of my life that they was filmin' me. I even changed my name. To Karla. Just to mess her up. I tell folks, you want a good time just look up ole Karla. And sometimes I give them her address.

17. A POETICS

...it is possible to evoke various contours of meaning by metaphorically considering the domains made real by various formal configurations.
— Charles Bernstein, *A Poetics*

Now preye I to hem alle that herkne... if ther be any thyng that displese hem, I preye hem also that they arrette it to the defaute of myn unkonnynge, and nat to my wyl, that wolde full fayn have seyd bettre if I hadde had konnynge.
— Geoffrey Chaucer

I never mentioned that my father is also an accountant. And look at us. Terrible with numbers, the odds are against us:

> You and me against the world. Sing it with me,
> Sometimes it feels like you and me against the world.

Your friend once said that as a student, you had a remarkable capacity to assess a complicated problem and break it into coherent parts. That you would remark, cryptically, "Someday, all my secrets will be known." Left to carry on, I am dismantling you, your secrets. Unpacking them, magnetized words in a box, and arranging them, this way, and that way.

The letters are mutating, although they have not changed in essence. Since I have abducted you, you seem to be someone else. Yet there is a part of you that is inviolable. Abduction,

the tentative and haphazard
tracing of a system of signification …
will allow the sign to acquire its meaning.
And this (is) an act of imaginative courage

Umberto Eco, *Semiotics and the Philosophy*
of Language

I am unsure of my half-assed theft,
my rendering of you
acquiring shape, purpose.
Yes, I have the courage of Patton.

Four Stars: Provocative, compelling.

I will have no cowards in my army, I will slap you senseless if you cry in front of these brave women. And continue, toward my destiny, to capture you. This way, on

plain recycled terracotta japanese lined yellow manilla orchid-bordered paper

postcards (hello Toronto is clean a good time wish you were here)

letter legal oversized coloured envelopes,   stamps of the Queen of the flag of
Nelvana,

slide across my tongue   NOT the eucharist   a HIT of acid,

(your face is burning).

I meant to explain. I apologize for the informality, the liberties I am taking. Now. Leslie Dick has observed — she is a critic, a private eye and I adore her

she unfolds

> *I'll be the biggest scar in your side*
> *I'll be the biggest dick that you ever had,*
> *Hey wanna die, hey wanna die*

into Love — that genre has a tendency to ossify, preserving or mummifying what a Letter is, a Poem, an Essay (and so on). So if these are "letters" they are spiders in amber. Words slipped into ghost-envelopes, unravelling their linens.

The subjectivity you witness is, of course, fluid. Science/fiction — polymorphic and alien. Without intention, to this point. Other than affect.

I saw you, as you know, walking ahead of me. You were so close I could hear you breathing. I watched and listened. To sounds of torture and invasion, your own and Homolka's voices, closing in for the kill. And I was fearless. As though the plexiglass that separated you from the gallery was a shield, one that was capable of deflecting, of annihilating sensation.

There is an analogue in pleasure which, once stated, supplements emotion. And pain. Watching blood course from the soles of your feet before you know you've been cut.

Writing you allows me to feel constructive, to know who you are, who I imagine you are. In multiple, a sheaf of letters stacked and cut into the shape of one man, making a chain. Hand in hand, this chain-gang of one, dispatched to dig ditches, fissures, in the narrative. Anger, loathing, compulsion, attraction, clinical distance, abstraction. Furrows carved with the arrow head, the blunt edges of the instrument.

Non-linear contours, irreverent exposition obscured by reverence. Textual play, critical labour, exegesis. Various formal configurations. Not one thing or another, yet it's all the same, still, and

> *I will kiss you when*
> *I cut up a dozen new men*
> *And you will die somewhat,*
> *again and again.*
> — Anne Sexton, 1969

18. MIRACLE OF THE ROSE

As sunflowers turn to the sun, our faces turned
— Jean Genet

That I may rise and stand, o'erthrow me, and bend
Your force to break, blow, burn, and make me new.
— John Donne, "Holy Sonnet 14"

The epiphanic motion of Hercamone's chains, each link blossoming into flower; the thorns that crown his head. Jean reaching to seize one white bloom: the motion of Genet's faith (there are no questions: when the face of Christ appears on the lake, you simply cross over in your craft, blessing yourself).

Writing against despair, I am writing toward despair, forging roses of steel.

Yet I am aware of your transformation. A bridegroom with layered yellow hair, the chain-store nautical wear: my horror of the ordinary, how hideous you are. Watching the sun rise in Hawaii, a pink lei around your neck, your gimlet eyes, somnambular.

beauty is the projection of ugliness

It is only when you begin to disassemble — Karla is missing, you are dressed in black like a thief, your hair variegated, marigold — that you begin to acquire beauty.

A beauty that incinerates the more you admit. Your repulsive crimes. That give off such a fragrance, of tropical flowers spilling from caskets, tiger-lilies, snap-dragons.

Your face acquiring a different shape, cheekbones high and curved, your mouth tranquil, violet, your eyes are lapis lazuli, in Marquis settings. Pale as opal, the sun's last shadow on the sea.

In prison you do not move but lie on your alabaster bed, like the Bound Slave, marbled grey. One arm raised against the pillow, the other pulling at your tunic, disclosing ribs that are sharp scimitars, a tease of chiselled hips.

Showing me the grotesque heart that resides below, pushing blood from its ventricles in exquisite beats. Imprisoned in these very bars, you never shall be free, nor ever chaste, except you ravish me.

19: Two Boy Scouts: Ted & Paul

Photographs: Ted Bundy's mother Louise holds her son's Tacoma, Washington Boy Scout uniform and points to its crest, her eyes in shadow (she holds her son). Paul Bernardo smiles with Steve Smirnis, his striped scout-scarf immaculate: he has acquired two rows of badges.

Paul knows that Ted was a Boy Scout too, that many killers were. He does not find it unusual: each morning when he wakes he turns inward and remains that way. As if he has gathered himself into a tent after carefully mooring the ties with wooden spikes. He understands that he has something in common with men he has never known, and ventures that they read their pledges differently. What their vow to do their best and duty meant to them. That a little tribe of boys gathers across time and space the way child-vampires surge into the night to meet in love and eclipsed light: casting long broken shadows to pledge *For the Blood is the Life.*

He remembers that Bundy talked in the third person, referring to an entity of some kind. Paul understands this as the failure of language. Anthropomorphizing compulsion: it occurs to him that radiant saints, or men locked in convulsion, have been beatified, exorcised. That misunderstanding illness is commonplace, and necessary. Here, in the interior of the exterior, he arranges his body into a lotus and creates

a contour against the void.

There was anger once: his life was ugly and cruel. He knows now that he stepped into his shadow: a foolish child who cowered in fear, who turned, becoming fearsome. Living without pity and with contempt. How the undead deride the living, how tenderly they lock together when, hidden from the sun, they cleave to the moist ceiling of the cave. Their dreaming wings unfolding, cling: a chain of black dahlias, a membranous rope of pearls.

Paul learned to use a compass and knife; he could make a sling, eleven different knots; he built a birdhouse, using his grandfather's saw. At the end of every meeting, the boys would clamour after Akela. When it was time to gather under the moon one boy would call *do your best*, and the others would respond, *do our best*. Paul fought often to be that boy, he would throw his head back like a wolf and sound his own oath —

To separate himself in anguish and conviction. And better them. He alone watched the moon shiver in retreat as the bats bore against its delicate face, beating it beyond the clouds; he saw that there was nothing there but the same stillness and solitude he rests in, pendant. When the night returns he listens for the motion, the rush of the nocturnal train.

20. KARLA'S SUICIDE-DESIRE

And there is a charge, a very large charge
For a word or touch
Or a bit of blood
— Sylvia Plath, "Lady Lazarus"

I hope they'll let me do my hair in jail. I would just die if my hair went all to hell.
— Karla Homolka

Dying is an art, Karla informs her new friends in segregation at Kingston's P4W. Like anything else, I do it exceptionally well. I do it so it feels like hell. She shows them her wrists, asking them to look closely at the faint white scars.

I did that when I was sixteen, with a razor-blade. It's easy enough to do it in a cell. But I will not do it again; I want to taste the spring, like

the Maids, the long royal lady bee.

But once, long ago, I couldn't see the point of going on.

I tried sleeping pills too: Sometimes I just don't want to live is what I told Susan. She was upset because I had so much to live for (even though her own wrists had deep vertical scars). She said I had really nice hair, which made me feel better for a little while but when I think back I know I was dyeing it all the time to show how I really felt. Red, black, and green, nausea, bruises, I was moody, you know? I didn't want people looking at me, I was all alone. I just wanted to read and draw my dream house. I have so many of those diagrams, it's pandemonium.

I wanted pink shingles and white lattice work. A pen in the back for Ariel, a nursery all done in sea colours, the ceiling covered in glow-in-the-dark stars and planets. A nice bright kitchen, and a beautiful bedroom — just pine — the sheers and coverlet pale blue.

I could see myself so clearly, mixing martinis and handing one to my husband. Feeding him the olive and listening to him talk about his day, our dreams. I imagined he was a prince who worked at an embassy and wore a golden crown.

I was all messed up. So I wrote this poem, "Suicide". And after I read it to Susan we decided we would never talk about it again:

> I'm thinking only of myself.
> But it's my life, isn't it?
> It is hard to take a life, yet so easy.
> Life is so fragile, yet so strong.
> It all depends on which way you want to go.
> I am caught up in this world, a nightmare.
> Only time will tell.

But I did talk about it again. I believed in the devil, that there was an evil in the world. Demons and curses, I could cut out with knives or lose, in a dreamless night that never ended. I became a lot happier after I met Paul and began to draw him into my diagrams.

Maybe he was the devil I was afraid of, Karla tells her friends.

When she is alone, later, she thinks, the devil would never stay in jail. He changes shape as it suits him: he could be this stuffed bear I am holding, the fires of hell raging under its button eyes. Or the water from my sink, if it pools in sixes; the fork I use for dinner, it is as black as pitch. It all depends on how you look at it; it's my body, isn't it?

My own body. Which will soon appear as mist by night. Into Paradise, myself changed. Dressed in reptile green and snakeskin, I will unfold my angel's wings.

Only time will tell what demons await, but I have assailed them, and will again. I will consider all things visible in Heaven, Sovereign of creatures, Empress of this fair world: I will taste all that catches this longing eye, tulip, orchid, hollyhock; all who come to steal a kiss, or gaze with rapture at my seraph's face.

She tells these and other secrets to herself, as she styles her hair into waves, listens to the curling iron hiss, as it clasps and splits each fragile lock.

POSTCARD: WITNESS FOR THE PROSECUTION

You have always dreamed about winning. You will be asked to fill out a preliminary form. Answer all the questions honestly. Dress appropriately for the meeting. Coaches certainly can be helpful. They can suggest reading material. To win the title, you have to want the title. You have to really want it. Remember, the judges are there because they want to meet you. One judge's criterion: she must be a woman of sound mind who can handle a year of abuse. Don't let your lips be lazy. Pronounce every syllable of every word. Show people that you love them, and they will love you back. Select your hairstyle well in advance. You cannot go wrong with a classic pump. Take advantage of every opportunity to perform before an audience. Do not discuss your interview with other contestants. Focus your eyes on the judge when you talk. If your eyes roam the judge will think you are not interested, nervous, lying. Sample question: "What does Women's Liberation mean to you?" Wear tasteful talent togs. Plan ahead. Poise is confidence and composure. One of the most awkward moments in your reign may be when the crown is first placed on your head. The press will not just quote the winner, they will quote people who knew the winner. Your family will be interviewed. Your neighbours, teachers, and childhood playmates may even be interviewed.

Fuckin' bitch is sicker than me and she only gets twelve years.
— Paul Bernardo

21. KRISTEN

She had bad dreams. She would wake up screaming and I would come to her; she would cry and tell me her dreams until she fell asleep again.

Some man is holding a knife to my throat, I was looking at a map except it didn't make sense. I lost my shoe.

I can't see anything but I hear a zipper opening and it's the man and he tells me to go down on my knees. I'm crying and he hits me and has sex with me.

He keeps making me have sex and I say no, and then he hits me.

I am trapped in a closet and can't get out and I'm sick, throwing up, and trying to pick the lock and it won't open.

He gives me my underwear back and someone brings in drinks. Tequila Sunrises. I'm scared you are worried.

I can feel blood everywhere.

I am pulled into a bathroom and he tells me to go and watches. I'm hungry. He steals the necklace my boyfriend gave me. I say that I hate him.

We sleep next to each other and I can't wake up. I can see a lady lying on the floor beside us and her eyes never close. A dog is barking.

He sings to me. That's a good song I say. He lets me have a bath and I try to wash him off the way I was throwing up before.

And the two of them make a movie that I'm in, touching them, and, and he gets mad again. Then I'm in the same bathtub except he's trying to go to the bathroom all over me.

He asks me to be in a beauty contest. I am in my school uniform, trying on different perfumes. Eternity, I tell him. I like that one.

I think, I'll do whatever they say and they'll let me go. I try to ask her to help me when he's gone. She doesn't say anything.

I hear Dad's voice. He's saying he loves me. That you are both praying I can come home. But I can't find him. My arms and legs are all tied up.

My mouth is filled with blood I can't breathe.

My shoe is lying beside the Grace Lutheran Church.

I know I can't make him happy, he gets angrier when I try.
I am locked in a closet and I can't get out. I can taste him.

The dog is crying.
I can't find you.
I am sleeping in a bed of branches by a creek.
I have no hair left or clothes.
The map I was looking at. It was of another city, not the one she said.
It didn't make sense.
I can't wake up, a different man, older, is kneeling beside me.
He lifts up my arm and I hold his hand and don't let go.
I have a daughter he says, and closes his eyes.
I know I am never coming home.

22. LOVEBIRDS

According to biographer Donald Spoto, Hitchcock chose taxi-
dermy as Norman Bates's hobby because he felt that the sexual
psychopath enjoyed "stuffing birds".

You were marred at birth by a blood clot which spread over your face like a
jellyfish. It made your mother sick to look at you.

A quiet and frail boy allergic to orchard grass elm ash poplar cotton, you
could not speak.

Your birthmark faded and surgeons excised the skin that attached your
tongue and palate, a sheet-web of flesh.

You became talkative and sweet to look at. Unlike your father, who hurt
your mother and made your sister cry at night, when no one was listening.

You and Karla had a special bond after Tammy died.

The way she died — it was unfortunate, a terrible accident. She is diffi-
cult and yells at you, but she would never hurt a fly is what her friends said,
and she cares for you.

Small girls, who eat like birds, visit and it makes Karla angry. She won't
speak of disgusting things because they disgust her.

The tin soldiers in your bedroom, the wooden blocks, Beethoven's *The
Eroica*.

Her refusal to go into the cellar, where the fruit is preserved, the way the
sun just illuminates her silvered head on the pillow.

You do everything for her and she betrays you. You wonder: Why is she
so mean to me? The presents you gave her in spun-gold cloth: pheasants,
crows, lovebirds.

She's the sick one, you say, and I'm in here. She killed those girls.
Reverting to silence, you don't want to talk about it anymore, just sit and
stare:

They know I can't move a finger, so I'll just sit here quietly in case they suspect me. They're probably watching me — well let them. They'll see what kind of person I am. I'm not even going to swat that fly! I hope they are watching! They'll see and they'll know, and they'll say "Why, he wouldn't even harm a fly!"

23. ABDUCTION

paul's novel: an excerpt

Then he told Lori about his "looping" theory. As Lori recalled, it had something to do with dying: people die but they do not really die, they keep living. He told Lori he was going to write a book. It involved spiders and all sorts of different things.
— Stephen Williams, *Invisible Darkness*

Or perhaps time flowed differently on Earth...
— Philip K. Dick

He would never remember why he had opened his eyes. He had been dreaming, having a nightmare about spiders. They were swarming him and binding his legs and arms in gossamer.

Many times, resting in his cage, he would try to reconstruct that evening. He had gone to bed late, and had fallen asleep quickly. Something made him sit upright, blinking. His face stinging, the phosphorescent light from their bodies, the smell of their skin. Castile soap and chamomile: he felt sleepy.

When he tried to open his eyes again he could not see. He was blindfolded, and strapped to a metal table. Prehensile limbs probed his naked body; he felt himself being mounted by sleek incremental shapes. He could not scream through the gag as the scalpels and electrical prods explored his flesh. His flailing hands captured a thin, coarsely textured tarsus before they were restrained with cuffs.

They led him, battered and bleeding, to a small enclosure. It would be many days before they removed his blindfold and gag. Scream all you like, they told him. It's up to us if you live or die. And he wanted to scream, to drop dead at the sight of them. He curved his body into the corner and tried not to cry. The Arachnids had beaten him savagely for this before. He tried to think of his life on Earth, of someone he had loved; he struggled to think of a way out, but he was helpless. When they began visiting him less, he became truly afraid.

Eventually the cage became filthy, and days would pass before one of the Aliens would bring him food. He would stare pleadingly into their bright black eyes. Sometimes they would stare back, their spinnerets quivering. Before baring their teeth.

He knew that soon they would stop coming at all, that he was no longer useful to them. He rationed his flies and moths, his rain water. His own body had become repulsive to him; he had lost his sense of time. Memories returned to him, feverishly. The sound of the spacecraft's doors, slamming behind him. Colliding with planets, the rings of Saturn, the shocking pink of Mars. A Nubian mummy he saw in a museum, curled up under glass, his shrunken hand raised to his mouth. He lay this way, thinking of time. How quickly it moved on Earth, that he could place his own hand against the mummified hand; they were almost touching.

Toward the end he thinks in colours and shapes, slow insectile thoughts, yellow spokes. Sunlight. In the window: he was a child and his mother was unpacking an orange fly strip. She hung it over the kitchen table and he asked her if it would catch spiders. I hate them, he said. The spiral strip took shape in his head, a diagram of infinity. Two loops intersecting, replaced each summer.

He sees himself, unsticking the spiders, tearing them apart. And watching them return again in time, crawling in the shadows, hanging on draglines, from cobwebs. Time will pass and he knows he will die. But he will not really die, he realizes, as his heart constricts. As he watches them, ensnaring him in silk threads, he is sure that he is falling through the spiral. To begin again, a still shape, sheathed in white, his blood flowing in darkness, after the first slap.

24. THE GRAND ILLUSION

In Grand Illusion ... the reticence of Renoir's camera is more than a beautiful tact. It is the refusal to assert what no one is in a position to assert for us: where it is that one man's life ends and another's begins. Or the refusal to manufacture a response, however sweet the complicated pain, which covers our complicity...
— Stanley Cavell, *The World Viewed*

Listening to the videotapes in court (Justice Patrick Le Sage has ruled that the gallery can hear but not see the films). The relentless music. The muffled sounds, a girl's voice: "I'm going to pee all over you."

Ice-T raps *Bitch* over and over.

Bernardo: I like that, I like watching girls urinate.

Reading graphic accounts of the rapes, torture, murder, dismemberment.

Screaming in pain, calling Help me.

Watching Bernardo demonstrate how he sawed through flesh and bone; Homolka watching herself, expressionless.

The saw jamming, its teeth caught. Homolka rinsing and disinfecting.

On film. Both Bernardo and Homolka have directed, though she denies she is the auteur. She directed and filmed when she was ordered to: she was afraid.

The hand-held camera is steady, producing clear images.

Afraid of this impassive man, a monster. Looking at them both, there is an absence.

Nausea and fear, experienced differently.

What distinguishes this trial is the videotape evidence, an unprecedented assault on the Not Guilty plea.

It is the filmic element of the crimes that deprives us of sensation. Even the killers, behind glass, restate this phenomenon. Of watching in suspension, detached.

It is film that governs the crime-literature: each extant book or article about the trial deploys cinematic as opposed to literary strategies.

Terror is achieved in this literature through careful editing.

The scene of the crimes must be revisited: it cannot be destroyed.

Thomas Aquinas: When you get to the heart of evil there is nothing there.

Like flinching before a blow; pressing your ears to the ground to hear the hooves and spurs of the cavalry from a distance.

Houlahan: The videotapes are worth a million words.

It's just a movie.

Burnside and Cairns: Kristen is seated, in part, in front of the hope chest on the floor.

Pron: A severed torso of a young woman is discovered in Lake Gibson. Cut to: The two newlywed killers stroll on the beach in Maui.

The Bernardos' Port Dalhousie home was recently torn to the ground.

Affect is always evoked through quick, narrative cuts.

A woman steps into a shower. Her expression of pleasure is broken by the sudden parting of the shower-curtain, the appearance of the knife.

The author must collaborate with the auteur.

Bernardo is called Captain Video by the prosecution; the Master, director.

Bernardo's films provide the locus for the (compounded) narrative. They are source-"texts," without which discourse cannot proceed.

Cavell: ...an aesthetic proposition even more unnoticeable in its obviousness, that a movie comes from other movies.

All accounts of the Kennedy assassination proceed from the Zapruder film. However impoverished or accidental, the original filmic document provides the foundation for all subsequent narratives.

Jackie Kennedy crawling *away* from her husband's body.

Authors and filmmakers must design their work, inevitably, according to the vision of the original auteur.

We liked making homemade pornographic videos, Sir.

Collusion occurs: Bernardo staged a beauty contest between Kristen French and Homolka (who was dressed in a schoolgirl's kilt). He filmed them lifting their skirts.

Stephen Williams recounts this event: through his lens Paul could see that there was no comparison. Karla was wearing white bikini underpants that bunched unattractively between her cheeks. (Williams adjudicates).

Bernardo's films do not recount the lives of the actors.

Authors attempt to provide this information as a coda to the films.

The actors/victims are imprisoned in the documentary, a genre which recounts without retelling, which is factual, not fictional.

A closed hermeneutic circle.

In *Blowout* and *The Conversation*, audiotapes are played backwards and forwards, obsessively, as though the documented events can be altered.

In film, nothing can be undone.

Bernardo is a bad filmmaker.

I do not feel for his actors.

Grand Illusion *is about the illusion of borders, the illusion that they are real and the grand illusion that they are not.*

The illusion has become real, how does it feel?

At night I imagine I am one girl, or another. How I would bite, kick, escape. I think of rescuing them, of bringing them home. Rigid with anger, I surrender. To sleep, knowing I cannot change what I fear, that their images can never be unlocked. They suffer forever, moving away from, and into despair.

My name is Leslie Erin Mahaffy.

I want to go home.

I'm really sorry for what I said. I shouldn't have said it.

My name is Kristen Dawn French.

Zeus's servants, Force and Violence, bound Prometheus to a rock in adamantine chains where an eagle devoured him for eternity.

His name...has stood through all the centuries...as that of the great rebel against injustice and the authority of power.

— Edith Hamilton, *Mythology*

25. John Rosen

Found Poem: "Bernardo Has Been Called"

The Best Boyfriend in the World
Philanderer two-timer Lecher
Son heathen Our weekend son

Stalker hunter Victimizer
Winer diner Whiner
Misogynistic narcissistic Hedonistic

Rapper cross-border shopper
Hissing insulting Sneering
Pornographer masturbator Predator

Awful hateful Brutal
Incredible unbelievable Unspeakable
Liplicker wormpicker Bruiser boozer loser

Infantile penile
Despicable dysfunctional Disrespectful
Heartless remorseless Infamous

Yelling grinning
Insulting self-gratifying Self-aggrandizing
The Worst Boyfriend in the World.

— But what he is not, members of the jury, is a murderer.

Closing Statement: August 28, 1995

26. Paul's Current Affair

"David" spoke eloquently and convincingly (to A Current Affair's Mary Garofalo) about his time living next to Paul Teale in Special Needs Unit 2A, the jail's segregation unit...while awaiting trial on charges of sexually assaulting a male prostitute.
— *The Globe and Mail*, December 4, 1993

David with the sling, I with the bow, Michelangelo.

I chose the name David because it reminded me of him. When I turned around he was there, just towering over me. Sculpted arms and legs, alabaster in black tank and shorts. His head raised and an angry look in his dumb eyes. I ordered him a drink and he let me touch him; I traced the tendons in his neck and he said I felt cold. I thought of filling my mouth with ice and kissing him, of spreading him in the snow to make an angel.

I showed him the green and he came home with me, but I was scared. The money did not belong to me. Then I started shaking, remembering Craig said he would break my arms this time, one at a time, with a tire iron, a hammer claw. I still had the eight-ball left, and I laid out some lines. We even had wine, a bordeaux I said would warm him up. And when he drank I saw his chest glow, like a ruby in white tissue, as if his heart was burning.

Blossom Dearie singing, *There's a trick with a knife I'm learning to do*, and this boy stretched out on the divan, his arm in repose. His eyes slitted, drowsy, framed by the gold spread. A single lily fell in a curve over his sweet head.

I asked him if he loved me and he smiled. Which upset me, so I asked again. I was agitated at this point, starting to think that he was laughing at me. I looked out the window and watched the pigeons cluster on the filthy ledge. And that made me think how birdlike he looked, his puffed chest and thin legs. That he was a filthy scavenger — I thought of him taking awkward flight.

Away from me. I asked if you loved me, I said and advanced, the wine bottle damp in my hands. I was going to pour it carefully, on his breast, feather of scarlet tanager, robin, cardinal lines of blood streaming from his forehead. I had broken the bottle and green glass was raining around us as I lowered his briefs, used its neck and edges to open him, plunging deeply inside, finding his heat. Later, I felt lost as though I died a little, and I held him and asked him again if he loved me.

The next thing I knew I was being manacled. He was gone, the police led me barefoot to the car, my feet brilliant with green glass — I left red footprints in the snow, which made me think of Nijinsky — a dancer who went mad, whose lover made him leap higher than dreaming, whose ravaged feet are the little red shoes of the ballerina in film, whose *grand jeté* calls her to death.

I talked about the ballet with Paul. We talked a lot because he was scared and lonely. He said his brother's name was David, that he liked movies and music. Something called *Use Your Illusion* — he said it's about November rain, about a bride who is killed. How lovely I thought that was, the image of the vestal white, the crimson of the sacrament.

I cut his hair for him once and it was soft, like a baby chick is what I told the woman who interviewed me. I watched him shower and then he came to me and said he knew what I wanted. He pressed against the bars and I took him in my mouth, careful not to bite. When he came I tasted dove soap and bitter endive. And I kissed him once, on that tender cleft at the base, I kissed him because I pitied him. He could never know what I want:

One who possesses such beauty that none may confine its spirit.

27. SURVEILLANCE

Bernardo's Kingston Penitentiary cell measures four by eight feet and is sealed with perforated bullet proof plexiglass. It contains a cot; a desk and television stand; a sink and toilet. A twenty-four-hour surveillance camera records his every movement.

You know what I want you to do.
— Bernardo to French, April 17, 1992

I need a better angle here Paul, you know what I want you to do. That's right, move your legs higher, that's good. Now swing them off the cot. Not like that, you fucking idiot, don't make me mad. I want you to stand up slowly. Are you scared? Just close your eyes and stand there, that's good. Okay, now walk over to the toilet and don't move, do what I tell you. Do you love me? Call me your mistress, that's right. Now unzip your fly and show me your cock. Don't make me mad, make me happy. Pull it out slowly and show me, lift your balls with your fingers. If you do it nice I may let you out. That's nice. Let your pants fall to your ankles. I said DO IT, you bastard. I'll hit you again if you don't...that's great. What are you crying for? Tell me you love me. You know what I want you to do. Sit down and take a piss like a girl. And tell me you love it, cunt. You're lucky I don't make you shit, but you look nice covered in your own piss. Get up. You won't get up? Well, I'll show you something, I'll show you what happened to the last guy I watched. Good, you're not so stupid, walk back to your cot. Don't lie down until I tell you. Listen to what I'm saying and I won't have to kill you. Lie down now. Show me that smile. Do it better, you fuck. Keep doing it and don't fuck me around. Lick your lips and keep telling me you love me, that's it slut. You're never going home if you can't, you fuckhead. You piss me off — open your mouth wider. Yes. Yes. Yes.

28. THE WORM-PICKER

On good wet nights ... the earthworms would come to the surface to avoid the seeping water...
— Burnside and Cairns, *Deadly Innocence*

You would go out at midnight and comb the fields for earthworms. Plastic pails strapped to your hips, flashlights seeking the slow slither of boneless bellies and banded tails. Gathering them in squirming handfuls you would sneak through the grass until the pails' mouths gaped, bloated from the sleek and sinuous weight of the night crawlers that bought you your first car. It was then you began to sleep through mornings, preferring to decelerate, edging through the streets. The soft yellow beam picking out motions, a skirt's swish, a shoe's quick skirl. Under the sallow streaks of a mackerel sky, you flexed your hands like hooks, in anticipation. Of all the nights you would steal through roads, hallways, riverbanks. Summoning movement, mesmerized: the segmented body, the sightless eyes. Compelling them toward you, tremulous and spellbound. Christ, it is believed, is best rendered as a worm. His radiant likeness unknowable, this infidelity to form a fidelity to its referent.

At midnight you come to the garden while the others dream; betraying your presence with a glow, you kneel and kiss the ground. And flush, seeing the golden shimmer, hearing its graceful sound.

29. THE LITTLE GIRLS UNDERSTAND

I'm a back-door man. The men don't know, but the little girls understand.
— The Doors

Shake for me girl, I wanna be your back-door man.
— Led Zeppelin

In high school you tried to figure it out. While your history teacher droned on about ancient Greece you thought about song lyrics, about being a rock star. Tossing your long hair as you learned to play "Smoke on the Water" on your El Dégas Les Paul copy (Christmas 1979).

You wanted to get laid very badly; you wanted something else. You got high with your friends, baptizing the Sensimillia rolled tight in tigerskins, buds popping. Set up a strobe light and thought about 12 strings, whammy bars, girls with little hearts sewn on the backseam of their jeans.

You knew there was a connection between ass-fucking and stadium rock, your eyes riveted to Robert Plant during *The Song Remains the Same*. The outline of his cock, Page thrusting against his guitar.

How beautiful they were, and dangerous.

Putting this behind you at some point, what was left was the idea that looking at her face was an impediment to what you needed. Hard slamming sex, no kissing, or worse, her eyes' reflection.

That's what's so heavy about you, man. You don't want any of the sentiment, just a dry blistering ride. I can dig it.

It's not like you are holding anything back (the waves of his blond hair, his rolling hips: that wide Sargasso Sea between you and any other bitch).

You wrote about "Stairway to Heaven" in your notebook, under the *ZoSo* rune, and made sense of it all one high day:

> Yes there are two paths you can go by
> But in the long run
> There's still time to change the road you're on

As you wrote out these lyrics from memory, you saw the May Queen, the Piper calling you to join him. And thought, as you took a hit from the bong, my shadow is taller than my soul.

Whoa — like, I'm being tailed by this groove, no matter what. It shows where I'm at, in a certain slant of light.

Somewhere in the drum lapse of "Moby Dick", you lie and reconfigure. Knowing that the little girls understand (much later, Karla will become absorbed by the poem "The Road Not Taken").

I like birds, you'll say: chicks. Listening to them sing from the branches, the first time you offer yourself to a man and tell him: This is what you want.

> *Yet knowing how way leads on to way,*
> *I doubted if I should ever come back.*
> — Robert Frost

30. The Revenger

I am your spiritual advisor. My name is Sister Catherine and I will come to you

a young man hot and vicious

though I still wear the habit. Black robe and wimple. The White Devil, Mother Superior said. She came to me at prayer: lashed to the spiked wheel, she broke her bonds and the stained glass shattered like thunderbolts. She rose and her merciful head was in her hands, milk bleeding from her veins. Sister, she said.

Adam of Saint-Victor has celebrated me, Saint and Martyr, of apologists, scholars, young girls, the wheels that set matter into motion: what I will ask of you.

Jeanne D'Arc has heard her singing   the Callas aria she sings to me. A ghost (my saint rising, bathing me in white), a play within a play:

> Christian: I embrace death and am myself still.
> The Cardinal: (Strangles her) Let us throttle the rest.
> Catherine: Cover her face; mine eyes dazzle. She died young.

And Madness. You feel that you are going mad, trapped in your cell. Let me comfort you, my child. I offer you this relic, a bone from the breast of Magdalene; come, confess your sins to me. The voices you hear are demons, you have heard them always. If you open your heart to Christ, He will be your Saviour, I implore you to accept Him.

What he whispers in my ear. I am soaked with his tears, as he feels the stone of sin dislodge and the Lord, in mercy and righteousness, appears.

I have seen Him, he cries. And he is radiant.

I am saved. He speaks with wonder, and falls to the ground. I fall with him, and speak quietly. About the fires of hell, the torment he will feel, as he is tied, screaming, to the catherine wheel that spins for all eternity, eviscerating him.

He is ashen, then angry. He does not speak as I hold the blade to his face and tell him.

I was a girl once. A man took me from the street, far away.
He brought me to the ravine and raped me until blood rained,
soaking us both. And left me to die. I watched the water
flowing past, colonies of ants. Carrying leaves like palm fans,
blessing me.

I am sick thinking about him; I want to throw up. I never left my home
until the day the ants returned. Dragging a string of rosary beads. The
colour of rubies and one pure ivory Christ. Nailed to a tree, I was scratching
at the tree and there was sap in my nails, green as his disgusting eyes and
wet filthy mouth. The wounds on His hands, Amen.
I listened to loud music my parents hated, as loud as I can scream

A VERY FINE RELIGION!

Jesus on his mare, smiting the wicked, O I'm talking about the Midnight
Rambler, the way I would creep out at night, and pour honey from a bear
into their hills and pray.
And pray and return to my room with the speakers thumping, stamping
on the floor

(my mother was inconsolable, my father never spoke of)

my childhood dead. And my long black and white hair, so Cruella de Vil,
whipping the air as I played along, on air guitar.
There's hardly any air left, is there.

       (pain I have never felt terror worse than falling
         fa ll ing into the water swallowing rocks
         sharp stabbing shamehorrorpain   )

I've got you wrapped up in my robes and you're smothering, no I won't
let that happen.

YOU RUINED ME

I'll say it was an accident like stepping on an ant, there's so many of them, you have to listen carefully to hear them break.

I'll step up now and let you catch your breath there is no light there isonly screaming.

I'll kiss your brow Judas, I'll stick my knife right down your throat baby, and it hurts.

31. ALGEBRA

Darren Tobin, an HIV-positive man who says he fantasized about the Paul Bernardo killings, told police he raped and beat a Good Samaritan because she kept talking about God... He said he has tried unsuccessfully to correspond with Bernardo and Homolka. "Blonde-haired girl, seen her a few times. I liked her a lot. But she was a bit sick..."
— *The Toronto Sun*, October 23, 1996

> Question: The attraction between two objects varies inversely as the square of the distance between their centres. If the attraction is 10 when the objects are 5 inches apart, find the attraction when they are 15 inches apart.

I studied algebra at night school, looking for women there too. I tested positive. I like the expression "full-blown" very much, as though I have been tined and seeded. I hope that it is an asphodel, I mean, when the buds push through me and blossom in their first thrush.

The answer to the question is 1 1/9. I thought of us five inches apart — you examining my letter — then 15 — putting it down unread. The current of attraction I had calculated between two persons, being you, and me, was diminished by your lack of interest.

I failed my term paper, which was predicated on a set of corresponding values, wherein our desire to kill was constant (h), and our relative lifestyles presented the variable (b). All of this was adjoined to the rectangular structure Darren-Paul. The final values multiplying and dividing our access as opposed to our intentions. I did further encode the constant (h) with a subset of variables which included penitence, death, and loss of will. My teacher said that my theory was without foundation. I told her that algebra is meaningless unless it is used to study actual problems.

Triangulation: your reading/crime, what I read about you. I know there are *a priori* theorems: you lying like Y over X = ordering that sick girl to blow you, and my arms crossed against the Samaritan. Forming an equation where time is represented by the line/horizon that separates us; there are no miscellaneous series of events.

She wouldn't stop talking about God (she wasn't the first). Jesus is on his way I told her. He will smite me with his sword and then he'll carry you through the walls and turn you into a beautiful dove.

Kristen and Leslie asking to go home, where you took them, in your sweet chariot.

Sodomy underlined in your paperback novels, my newspaper clippings about you and me: by the power of three times three (1/9).

I would become the garden I remember, in Cartierville. My grandmother's backyard. A sloping hill, creeping along a fence, flowered. Tulips, iris, rhododendron. The pattern of her skirts. When I would pull away there was an impression of leaves and vines on my cheeks. Becoming thin, her bones and body come undone — sweet feelers that pull me below the graph-lines (your matrix of bars), into the soil that is inside me.

A disease. Mathematical intricacies, germane to biology: viral behaviours, neurons aligning sexual pleasure and violence. Problems I never solved: I was looking for women, and found them.

I hurt them terribly, but you never responded.

Flora, Pansy, Daisy: they lie and wait for their stalks to bend, jaundiced, under the gaudy weight: rank petals, falling away.

32. FOUND POEM (2)

Be a perfect girlfriend for Paul.
Remember you're stupid;
Remember you're ugly;
Remember you're fat.
Save yourself. Kill them all.

— Excerpts from Karla Homolka's self-improvement list, fall 1987

33. TRIPBOOK

— was just looking at Paul's face & started this bummer which I thot I could end by concentrating on rainbowrainbowrainbow the acid I took w/window pane two hits keep feeling the cat's violence & uncool eyes as tho he's put a spell on me like that tune I don't care if you don't want me cause I'm yours anyhow. I was drawing peace signs & they came out occult & I'm looking to the north for that mother/earth & real power, you dig, goodness. Holy, holy, everything's holy but his lips are moving saying unreal things to me, man I can't listen to this, I've got to pull the tacks out. Carefully. Wrap him up, like bind him against whatever pocoloco bad juju he's got going on. Yeah, I got him in a silk bag now his voice all muffled, something like You know me, I'm yr friend. I'm shaking all over & I'm pulling out this picture of Christ where he's just getting down with all these babies & sheep & his mild eyes are these farout wells where I'm cleansing myself & my old man just put on Al Green. A heavy tune about Jesus. Is waiting, when yr broken down. This part, check it out, he goes, I just want to say I'm sorry sorry sorry. This sister said to me some time ago that I don't know how to get around evil, I just climb in. She's witchy & wise, saw me unclean & said, you know, blow it off. Like dandelion spores, when you wish for love & I'm sitting here freaking out & low-creeping in lakes of fire. I just want to say this evening, that I'm sorry, say that to this righteous face looking so sad for my sins & waiting on me, I'm sorry —

POSTCARD: WHILE THE OTHERS SLEEP

I refer to myself as Serge when I am having the daydreams. Of acting out my crimes while the others are sleeping. I am a deadly innocent French man named *Serge, âllo, salut, je m'appelle Serge, ma belle.* These girls are what you call witches, yes? I think I am having the hallucination but *non, non,* there she is. *Chérie* would you like a little cigarette, *ah bien. Oui, Gitane.* This is what I smoke: it is *brut* like me, oh, *petite fille.* Don't cry. This is no good. I will not allow it. Where are you going? *Chienne!* I am a big recording star of the rap music, *une étoile.* I am driving in my Peugeot, growing a little moustache and thinking fondly of Paris, ah slapping my girls and then the kisses! Officer, no you are not mistaken, *j'ai tort.* I was speeding just a little and I heard your amusing siren, *merci.* The others are sleeping in their cells and I am somewhere else. *Une autre ville,* my mind is not captive, make no mistake: it is the *Arc de Triomphe,* overlooking the city of lights. At its base is me, handsome and Gallic, charmingly still. There is always the rain, deriding those lovers without berets, when they turn their faces down and imagine they are crying it hurts them so, they are crying *brumes et pluies,*

my eyes are clouds that accumulate moisture, that darken the skies.

34. WHOSO LIST TO HUNT

I don't know how you found me. My name was never released to the public. And I prefer to be called Jane Doe now. Running faultlessly from the hunter's blind.

I am studying science. A correspondence course. I am an empiricist, which is interesting when you think about it. Each week I assert who I am, a letter in an envelope folded twice so there is only white.

She's just a plain Jane, you might say. If I was sitting right in front of you, as you looked intently for signs of damage. Finding nothing. My clothes are clean, there is a smell of lemons, vanilla. Plain blank face.

You have no idea — this girl was raped, I have read about it. And I can't help you. I have no recollection of this event. I could say that, becoming sleepy, I smiled at Karla and she touched my face. Angel heart, she said. The movie we were watching. I thought of her, my beautiful friend, in a headdress of chicken feathers, pulling my sweater up. (It's warm in here.) She made my

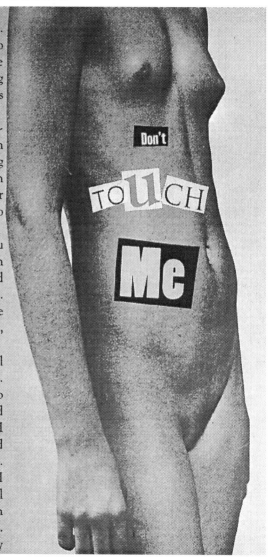

heart beat faster. I tasted blood in my mouth.

This would be a lie.

The next day I felt some pain and discomfort; something I ate, sleeping in an awkward position. It could have been anything. Why don't you ask someone else?

I live in a secluded house where there are deer. I read and look out the window. They reach up and pull leaves and bark from the trees. Sometimes they look back at me, I can't tell them apart.

I do not get attached to them. I have to underline things: my memory is poor.

You said that you were a writer. I have an interest in poetry, occasionally. Metaphors: the application of some thing or action, to an entirely different thing or action (with no emphasis on comparison).

Sometimes I am moved to tears by a certain song, an illogical construction: I forgot to remember to forget you. Because her loveliness made me ache, because she gave me things.

Events I did not experience, her own invention.

I want to give it back to her and you can't help me. If you could, I would ask you, like her, to write me.

Into a poem — I would leap from Karla's arms, my diamanté collar glittering. Behind me, she will falter, knowing to touch me not.

I am wild for to hold, though I seem tame.

POSTCARD: MAKE YOUR MOVE

you've got to fucking make your move
— Paul Bernardo

The table is spread with cards and poker chips. You are inscrutable: green visor and straight gaze. I am uneasy, holding the Dead Man's Hand.

I have been looking at you for too long, looking for clues — your face exhausts me. We are listening to the radio: Five Card Stud.

My stomach tosses; the boilermakers you insisted we drink. Beer with whiskey, submarine. You put all your chips on the line. I came here flush, and you could ruin me.

I want to fold. Spineless, I want to turn over. In green felt squares, and slide into your pocket. You see this in my eyes; my eyes are wild. And your mouth twitches, at the corner.

I call your bluff. See you and call. Black aces and eights I say; you slap down your pair of twos. You throw your car keys on the table: kings and little ones, you say. And I deal again. Queens high in my sleeve: I can't let you get away this easily.

35. THE INTERIOR

When the lights go down, the institutional silence falls. Ears prick up. The measured step of the guards, the moaning and crying. And close, like pink shells filling with clear blue water. Moving into dreams, the captives are as still as whales. Drawn up on the shore to kick their tails and fall, soundlessly, on broken flukes. Sleeping with one eye open, betrayed.

In the sea, the inmate stripes of black and white signal danger. They slide quietly through rock caverns, fields of red coral. Their occasional need to kill is not alarming. A sudden lunge, always from the back, and the blood flows like night tide. Colouring the stones, the opalescent bodies of keyhole chichlids, who look on, without blinking.

When they dream, they are these monsters. Swift, elusive, they break the barrier with their backs, enlarging the ocean. On shore, we stand in nervous groups, knowing not to touch their teeth, designed like razors. Wanting desperately to push them back, or carve out their mouths, tear away a dorsal fin, to remember them. What made them, how they have come back to us by accident, an act of mercy.

Their dreams are jangled. Battering a newborn baby with brute force, holding its head to the floor and filling its empty spaces until it is gone. Stealing through the dark passages where nervous pink salmon gather, ripping them to shreds. Listening, for the currents of distress and following them, electric with hunger. To capture terror, thrashing, between their jaws, and push harder, sleepless with need.

Hooked into the air and deceived, they were made of water. Formed to kill, a memory of conical teeth emerging, slipping from the interior of their own sleek mothers. If they were born as angelfish, they cannot recall. What impulse deformed them; they stare at beauty with wonder. Bright, exterior, they pare it to the bone to discover its radiance. And do not find it. Stuck in the night sand, they strain at the stars, maddening and arcane, shining beyond their sight.

36. THERAPY

While testifying, you said you thought you might need to seek professional help, and everyone laughed. I never did Paul; I want to help you. Through therapeutic art, you could express your feelings, good or bad. Clifford Olson, the serial killer (west of Kingston) writes poetry, and this has enabled him to dream of beauty. He writes about love and children; the Canadian Shield; the way the Prairies look on a hot clear day. Like looking into infinity. Killing, Elliott Leyton writes, is a deformed act of creativity. Once incarcerated, this talent can be reformed. Susan Smith, after being imprisoned for murdering her children, cried until she was placed on suicide watch (like you). She has begun drawing:

I do not know if you are artistic, but I believe that any imaginative act is valuable. The crude stick figures that parents tape to their walls; sketches on napkins you keep because you are sweet on someone.

In order to assist you, I will block out a sketch. A simple word construction, like Smith's MICHAEL (her son's name; he was an angel). And you can slash it out, as she has; fill in the edges and decorate it with sad or happy faces; lines and curves; even a sky and clouds.

Remember how you used rainbow and heart decals to mark your video collection?

 TAMMY

We'll begin like this, as collaborators. Finish what I have started:

I WANT TO DIE

POSTCARD: FATIMA

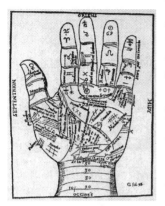

Your hand is very revealing. Where did you see me advertised? Yes, I have distributed many of my pink billets, on the wings of snow-white doves, lashed to the masts of small ships. Palmistry is not my first love I am afraid. I am afraid. Of this diagram you see, carved into sections as though I were a butcher. Phrenology. Yes. My clients would rest their heads on satin pillows and close their eyes, and I would make a noise like an Indian flute. Touching them, feeling the bumps and ridges, often scars. It is a lost art, one which I mastered. A curving slope, I would prophesy disaster! Boys tangled in their skis, metal poles impaling their hearts. A girl's constellation of mounds, detectable only by my fingers which I sandpapered to sheer satin, love. Embracing on a balcony in Spain, and the toreador presents her with the bloody ear of the bull. Bowing, and the swirl of his cape is like the evening breeze in — Your hand. You have had difficulty in love, love has tortured you. Even through this barrier I can see the cross-hatching, love's yearning met with hatred. Though gifted with numbers you lack a certain intellectual power. Your life will not be long, your fate is well-defined. Will it astonish you to know I see your childhood, painted like a Canaletto on your palm? There is the grass where you lay, crying, from hunger and fear. And the pony, Juliette, who bit your face, the dead birds you picked from the nest, still in their eggshell. In a pear tree, hidden from sight, you watched and waited. For nightfall. And the girls would rest before their windows, in slips and transparent robes, before pulling the blinds. This anguish — if I could touch your head, just once. Your brown hair like the earth and my fingers, pulling at seedlings, tangled roots. You would become sleepy, and I would regard you like a baby. The exquisite statue of the Madonna, holding her dead son. A madman took an axe to this, many years ago. He said that pure beauty is terrible, awful to behold.

37. SUCKER-PUNCH

Sex killer Paul Bernardo can barely see out of a cut and bruised left eye after he was "sucker punched" yesterday. Long-time thief Carl Bradley Hiltz became a hero to inmates at Kingston Penitentiary when he slugged Bernardo as he was being escorted back to his cell after his morning shower.
— The Toronto Sun, December 7, 1996

December is over and I have a bleeding ulcer: Paul, you're giving me an ulcer. Why can't you just stay still until I'm done? It makes me crazy. Looking at the newspaper again, thinking about this guy surprising you with a right hook, and your eye described as just about hanging out of its socket. He had befriended you too, spent some time in the segregation range, right after they found the razor in your cell. He told you about the big rigs. Climbing in, hot-wiring and putting the hammer down. Just flying: sixteen counts of grand theft auto. All the other prisoners high-fiving him. Rapists, murderers, skinheads — straight shooters. And then I get to thinking about Karla and her friends in P4W, all of them crocheting and making small talk, and I feel that reckless anger again. I mean, these are some tough broads. Knife-wielding child-killers — what is their problem? And there you are, it says, having mop water and urine thrown into your cell, and Hiltz just breezes up to you, unescorted. They're all in on it Paul, I don't want to scare you. They pave your food with ground glass and look away. It's an informal execution and no one's invited. And now they've got you pegged for the Elizabeth Bain murder: someone remembers seeing you seven years ago, searching for her body, acting strange. They'll just keep pinning this shit on you like Kick Me signs until the files are cleared and you appear dead in the exercise yard. Nobody saw anything. It was an accident. These kinds of things happen, and what the hell do you mean they have implications. This sick bastard has a television.

You're watching an infomercial with one eye. It's advertising a collection of love songs. You listen to the Commodores, thinking about sailors. Tying ropes into overhand knots, rescuing each other in semaphore. Each man to his place, they call. He was my friend, you think. You cover your face with a pillow and choke. Why is everyone so mean to me?

38. THE AVENGER

I work undercover in order to escape detection. I have many enemies, even from within. Gloria from Archives says that my reports often read like how-to manuals. She abhors violence but has remarked that my constant evocation of brand names functions as a conceit, murder as consumerism, the ends of invidiousness.

> Suspect A was apprehended at Harrod's. She was wearing a red Gaultier suit and red suede Manolo Blahnik pumps. Tiffany diamonds, Joy perfume, Chanel lipstick: Diabolique. After she resisted arrest, I gagged and subdued her with a pair of Donna Karan (extra-sheer) hose.

That sort of thing.

I received my mission today. Scrawled on onionskin paper — PAROLE. I swallowed the message and began plotting. I chose not to discuss this delicate matter with my male colleagues, who tend to be sentimental.

To pack:
Clothing
Boots
Map
Makeup
Rope
Razor
Cigarettes, matches
Identification
American Psycho

I swallowed this list also before departing for Kingston, Canada. On the long flight I drank Bloody Caesars and re-read her file. I thought about her saying, to the police, that she looked at the dying girl. She said: *I think I watched...like, what the hell, she's dead already.* I remembered her showing the agents the cellar where she had dragged the victim, stopping, and asking if she could have some of her things back.

I made precise notes: Hideous Beaver Canoe sweatshirt, cheap blonde hair, makeup by Revlon. Vain and highly intelligent: **proceed with caution.**

I looked at the autopsy photograph of her sister. A child with rumpled hair, her eyes closed. A livid chemical burn covering half of her face and mouth. Someone capable of unspeakable rage has smothered her, has

> *in heat/Of that ambition bloodily rushed in,*
> *Intending to depose (her).*

Sleeping above the ocean, *The Revenger's Tragedy* folded open in my lap. On my Harris Tweed suit beside my Hermés handbag. I dream that she and I are twins. I play tricks on her and steal her beaux; she attends my biology classes, expertly dissecting frogs.

I present myself to the prison matron as a representative from her university. My identification is in order, and she and I are led to a little room. She discusses herself and her studies and I listen. Stockholm Syndrome, Compliant Victim, Pluto and Minnie Mouse.

Do you think I'm pretty?
Yes, I think you're as pretty as a Spice Girl with twice the nerve.

I am applying Adventurous Wine to her lips, Marine Escapade on her cheeks and brow. I backcomb her hair with an Ilise Heitzner Harris comb, and style it with Aveda Pure-Fume Humectant Pomade.

She makes a moue and closes her eyes. Kiss me.

She waits and opens them and I have changed.

I am wearing my skintight black leather suit and boots. *Who are you?*

She is trembling. My name is Emma, Emma Peel. Now don't make a sound, I tell her, revealing the Aramis straight razor.

I disable her with a few well-placed blows to the neck, strip her down and hog-tie her. Referring to a page torn from the book she kept on her bedside table, I slice off her vagina. I love symmetry, and this woman is like white nylons and black shoes, dreadful.

When she moans, I light a Silk Cut and burn I CRY into her chest. And stuff her snatch into her mouth. Lick that, darling.

After a quick wash (*Je Reviens* soap in a sienna carrying-case) and change of clothes (Issey Miyake shift), I am off. I stop at the nearest safe telephone and say, It's over. My boss seems alarmed, claims he hasn't any idea what I'm talking about. Listen mate, I've done my job, I tell him. And devoured the instructions. It was sheer fucking graft, so don't make me answer to you.

Yes Emma, yes. Is what he always says. When he sees me in that black number, reaching for a whip. Oh Emma, yes.

39. A Hell of a Woman

Although Bernardo was undoubtedly a sexual psychopath with sadistic tendencies,
killings did not appear to be part of his paraphilia.
— *Invisible Darkness*

I'm not mad at you. I'm mad at the dirt.
— Joan Crawford

I like to lick little girls.
— Karla Homolka

Jane and the other one, January Girl or whatever, were one thing Paul. But I did not get married to come down here and find you using my best wedding crystal FROM FRANCE on this little brat. Put those away this instant. I don't give a shit if you're sorry, just bring her upstairs when I'm ready. And she'd better be clean. You are wrong if you think I'm going near her otherwise. No I am not Mad at you. She looks alright in a babyish way — That's it doll, just get me off, oh Christ that's good. Would you hurry? I'm not keeping her here, you can forget it. My parents are coming and I have not defrosted one single thing. Just get it over with. Oh yeah, that's great, big boy, great. Now warm up the car, I'll be down in a jiff. Here's a nice toy bear for you. Now I'm just going to kneel on your back. You're so wasted you won't notice. Stop moving! There now. Well I am truly sorry but she just died, what the hell was I supposed to do? Stick her in the cellar for all I care. I don't want her anywhere near my canned goods, figure something out, and I'll help you tomorrow. It's going to be clean though, I'm warning you. I have to take off work so you'll do this right, since you're useless. Great. My mother wants some potatoes. I'll do it. I have to do everything around here anyway —

2

Yeah, you get attached to these people. Especially the gorgeous ones. But I am trying to keep our lives together. Clean the house, go to work, and keep myself looking good. I mean, it's ridiculous. And he wants her to sleep with us like we're running a commune so I have to watch her all night. What am I, a dog? It gets easier anyway. I felt pretty bad the first time. Even though I wanted Tammy dead, I didn't exactly. She kissed my boyfriend; she was always in the way — I didn't do it on purpose Paul! Yes I do know how to administer Halothane, my hand slipped, ok? You just head off for some food, that's right honey. I've got the mallet, Christian's tied up. What could happen? Christian, Kristen, whatever! Oh sweetheart, I'm crying because she tried to get away and strangled, it was awful. It was awful when she tried to get away and I had to smash her face in. Now there's blood all over my hope chest, just more cleaning for me. Someone tried to prove all this with forensics, but nobody cared. I look so soft and white. It's Paul who has the face of a killer, Ray said so. In court and he said it really loud.

40. ASSLICKER

I'm your little cocksucker, cunt, slut, asslicker, and I want to marry you.
— Karla Homolka, letter to Paul Bernardo, 1988

My friend had a dream where he brought Karla to a party. She had just been paroled, and everyone was staring at her. Leave her alone, would you, he said.

She brings that out in you; she's so smooth and compliant, so fragile. The blue eggshell I keep in a glass box, retrieved from a tangle of grass and dandelions.

You may love actual women, but when you want to get off, there's nothing better. Than the one-dimensional kind, a letter to the editor —

> Dear *Real Affairs*, I was taking a commercial flight to Winnipeg and this luscious blonde stewardess

— or two or three, lined up with their skirts lifted, tumbling below you moaning, while you inflame them with your fingers, your snaking tongue.

After she confessed, a terrible burden was lifted from her pitiful shoulders. In Brampton, she Max-Factored, squeezed into a little black dress and went to Oscar's on Queen. She danced under the flickering neon, a red cat's face, Restaurant, Bar. After a few drinks, a stranger brought her home and they were intimate.

Then the naked pictures began arriving. While he read the morning papers, he looked at them, alternately. A very bad girl, he thought. Regretfully, as he tucked them away. She had sucked his feet, after letting her long hair fall slowly down his chest. Her body looked the same as it had, when the moonlight poured over her arched back, her long swan neck.

He did stop seeing her, after all. He read that she liked girls, and he had no idea how to introduce her to his friends and family. My little cocksucker, he thought, smiling. As he shut the drawer, and began calling everyone he knew.

41. The Battered Wife

You beat her with a flashlight, Paul. She looked like a raccoon. They are always looking for garbage; they are frightened by sudden noises.

You hurt her and that was wrong. The statistics are staggering. She knows this.

Don't ever hit a woman.

Some of them don't get mad.	(Load the Winchester and approach his unconscious body)
They know enough to be quiet.	(Don't snap a twig, just keep approaching the car where he has passed out)
They're sick of the torture, broken.	(Aim for the temple)
They fear for their lives.	(Fire until his brain exits through the back of his skull)
They have little self-esteem.	(Jane Stafford committed suicide in the Maritimes in 1992, years after executing her abusive husband, Billy)
They are irreversibly damaged.	(Karla has implied that she is more of a victim than Mahaffy or French)
They get even.	(*I think of this prison as a college dormitory; I look forward to working with women like me*)

42. My Little Sister

I felt totally terrorized. I did not feel I had a choice.
— Karla Homolka

I loved it when you fucked my little sister. I loved it when you fucked Tammy. I loved it when you took her virginity. You're the King. I love licking your ass, Paul. I'll bet Tammy would have loved to lick your ass. I loved it when you put Snuffles up her ass. I felt proud. I felt happy. I felt horny. It's my mission in life to make you feel good. I'm glad you made me lick her cunt. You know I had fun doing it. You know I liked it. We like little girls. If you're gonna fuck them, then I'm gonna lick them. All the little girls. The girls should be thirteen. I think you should fuck them and take their virginity. Break their hymens with Snuffles. They're all our children, and I think you should make them ours even more. I'm your cunt-licking slut, the keeper of your virgins. And I love you. I want to marry you.You fucked my little sister. And I let you do that.
— Karla Homolka, January 1991

Little Playtoys

> *(Tammy) was our little playtoy.*
> — Karla Homolka

Male reclining, made of soap.
Yellow star, taped to a drinking straw (a fairy's wand).
Clay figure: a woman with red hair and a green dress.
Crayoned leaf, purple.
Wooden hand, inked in red and orange spirals.
Blue robin's egg.
Plasticine head, with a ruffled base.
Ink house, on fire.

Today I dropped the clay doll and her head fell off. It was supposed to be me. I have been careless, with the things children have given me.

The little girl I love — she saw that I was tired and climbed on the back of the couch and we fell asleep.

She dreamed of the necklace I gave her: it was in a small box and covered in white fluff, the most beautiful jewels.

Staring at the dead wolves in the museum, sitting to look closer. Later, crawling behind the restaurant counter and coming back, covered in jam.

Bathing in a sink, smiling.

I hold her feet in the lake. She is wearing a pink sun hat and frilled suit. Her toes curl.

She calls out I love your hair, on her way upstairs.

A boy sits very close and she takes his hand.

When we sing to her she covers her ears.

One day old, her head is pink and blue.

She frowns when she makes things; she is never scared.

Broken toys are ugly, she thinks.

I am piecing this together, shell to star, Sophia. You are rushing to me, arms outspread. I can feel your weight, your fingers closing.

My mouth is filled with knives.

I feel my ears lay flat, I hear inhuman sounds. Someone who would hurt you is gone.

He has done it before. I have been careless.

Putting things away and when they break I remember *you can't be hurt anymore*,

I remember Doug French, saying this to his daughter.

MY LITTLE SISTER

My first boyfriend was cruel; I have a little sister.
She breaks my things and I am blamed for her mistakes.
Her hair is yellow, I envy her.
Sleeper duckling-yellow, its big feet push through the crib slats.
I am making a cake and she tries to help.
She ruins everything. I yell at her and put her outside.
She cries. To come inside, she cries in her sleep.
Sleeping, my mother has set her hair.
An urchin of crossed pins, white nightshirt.
Her feet are inverted, little ducks' feet.
She hurts herself and I run barefoot to her.
I close my eyes when the doctor pulls
the gravel and glass from her knee.
There is a white scar, a crescent moon.
I tell her I hate her, I am alone and sick.
She rests her head against me.
You are my best friend, she says.
She has admirers, a calico wild cat.
My hands are all pins and needles she tells me,
afraid she is sick.
She is afraid of noises, anger. Everything is alright,
a little girl. My boyfriend dislocated my arm,
he had a knife. Kicks, my ribs, I loved him.
The way my sister loves a boy who died:
she smashed a bottle that day.
She wears a piece of blue glass around her neck.
I heard her call his name. Once
I punched him in the face a black eye
and left him, he is still the same.
I tell my sister. Who is grown up, still little to me,
more radiant than the sun rising yellow
dress and shoes: her audacity makes me shy.

A man has never hit her, she is smarter than me.
Don't talk to strangers Mary. Her blue eyes
faultless, injure me
with their beauty. I mistake them, enviously, for my own.

43. SCREAM

for Dorothy and Lori Homolka

the families of the victims had to be counselled
        Susan Physick the victim-witness counsellor was familiar with terror
and was recognized
later   for her conduct   (given the Amethyst Award)

        the families would have to listen to
their children being raped and tortured   she held their hands she guided
them through this

like Charon: the boatman on hell's river:
        there is a boatman riddle, about a girl's murder
no one other than the murderer is to blame   but there are degrees
of culpability

the woman who watched and felt helpless   the man that would not
take her the man in

the van
        those who suspected and did nothing

the sister and mother of the woman who watched
        who sat in the courtroom with their fingers jammed in their ears

while the families of the girls listened   to the sounds of their daughters
                        screaming

44. ARGUMENT

Everything's too clear, with a clarity pointing to the desire to evade.
— Mallarmé, *Igitur*

Four Pieces

1. Scarborough
2. The Cat Burglar
3. Kidnapper
4. Through my confessions in my anguish —

About what follows:

After midnight, Paul Bernardo packs his rape kit (a knife, twine, a gag) and begins stalking women on the streets of Scarborough, a neighbouring city of Toronto known for its strip-malls and rock formations (the Bluffs). Vacant lots, alleyways: tracking the old spaces. He is in his early twenties, and his violent sexual urges have accelerated: he was the neighbourhood voyeur at a very young age. He rapes repeatedly, following a similar pattern. Striking the women, demanding oral sex and sodomy. He recites the familiar litany, *tell me you love me*. He does not kill them. Eventually he becomes a smuggler and a thief, enlisting the assistance of his wife, Karla Homolka. He beats Homolka and requires oral sex and sodomy from her for gratification; soon he will kidnap and rape young girls, enlisting her help. She defers because her safety depends on her cooperation. Random backhands in the car, the request that she degrade herself. His indifference. Nothing remains of their intimacy. He has evolved, he says, in his sexuality. The conflation of torture and unrequited love an absolute. His reckless life grounded in an early knowledge of illegitimacy. The girls he has captured cry and are not compliant. Madness without purpose. His ideas are threatened. One girl calls him a Bastard. He is consumed with rage and completes the cycle. Acquisition and exchange. *Give me the knife; I'll kill her now.*The woman he loves deserts him. He is infantile in his grief, his anguish. He wishes he had looked at her face and says so with what breath remains. His life begins in avarice. It concludes this way, thought and action soldered. There is grief and denial: *But I didn't kill these girls.* Prove.

Dig into all that

45. En Attendant Linc

(Julie) had developed a strong crush on him and often bemoaned...the fact that Paul was so cute and "damn it, why does he have to be married?"
— in *Deadly Innocence*

I resume alas alas abandoned unfinished...
— Samuel Beckett

Act I

A suburban living-room. A bathroom. A bedroom.

Evening.

Julie, slumped in a chair, is finishing a drink (Cointreau, Kahlua & Irish Cream). Her eyes are closed. Her head droops, nodding in time to the music. It is the Varsouviana. There is a gunshot.

Enter Paul.

Julie: This is the polka they played the night the boy I married — turn the light off!

Paul: (Prosaic) This is Body Count. (Passionate) Come on come on make some noise.

Julie: Let's go to the powder room where it's quiet, honey lamb. I'll light a candle and we'll kiss only once, softly. Let me find my wrap. Oh sugar bring me another of those sweet sweet drinks, they make my mouth water so.

Paul: (Winking) Let's go.

Paul and Julie enter the bathroom, lock the door.

Julie: Why, is this your wife's toothbrush? I swear I would like to put poison on it and have you all to myself. Aren't I wicked?

Paul: I think it's erotic.

He begins removing Julie's clothes and licking her body, slowly, from the neck down.

Julie: Oh — Tiger. Unhand me. Please. (As if to herself) It's so divine in here I shall pretend that there are fairy-lights, that you are a police officer who has shamelessly professed his love for me. A strong Black man

Body Count is playing distantly: *She went wild in a backstage bathroom, sucked my dick like a motherfucking vacuum*

with a stern face and afro paling only a paper moon. But it wouldn't be make-believe if you believed. In the slick part in my long blonde hair, my cool face and holster, Linc, Linc. Just tell me I'm solid, like that. No more words. Solid.

Paul: (Continues licking her body as she sits on the sink, her eyes still closed) We've had this date with each other from the beginning!

Julie: (Their exertions break the mirror) I'm in danger! Linc— (Paul mounts her: Mark, Kevin and Marlene listen at the door) Oh, harder, harder!

Julie has begun to vomit. She pukes all over him, all over the floor, and he continues until he is spent. He pushes her aside, reaching for the door.

Paul: I feel a glow.

Julie staggers to the nearest bedroom.

Enter Mark.

Julie: (Cries out) Fuck me up the ass. Paul, Paul —

Mark: Give your head a shake, woman. (Ejaculates).

It is morning. Julie is staring at her hands, alone on the rumpled bed. Karla is heard in the background, scouring the bathroom, hissing.

Karla: Just get her out my house. I could kill her.

Julie: (Frightened) Who are you? You are not Mr. Paul Bernardo. I don't know you. I've forgotten something. (Shouts) I have forgotten everything. And I feel like I am about to die. (She dresses quickly, in a sweat-suit and tiara.) A beautiful dream. That's all it was. (Dancing in circles, arms raised). There is pain but I have such feelings. I have filled my empty heart with mystery, illusion. He came to me in the darkness, yes, it was a stake-out, and we were filled with such need.

The background voices become louder. Someone is calling, Julie Julie, come out.

Mark: Julie, come out. You look beautiful, a real queen. (He smiles, licking his lips).

Julie: Whoever you are (Body Count is heard, faintly, *she said I love you*, she motions him away), you cannot understand. There is death in this place, the sheets are stained with blood. I don't tell the truth, and if that is sinful — Don't touch me! I am damned.

Mark retreats, leaving Julie standing in the doorway, her eyes searching.

> I am damned to remember nothing but the terrible terrible sweetness of Paul's mouth in shadow, enveloping me. The broken glass, my body eliminating what I did not want, my knees clenched

as I came. A little death. The opposite (Julie is blanched in faint morning light), the opposite is desire.

Curtain.

POSTCARD: RACCOON EYES

You are beautiful. Is how it begins. So beautiful. Especially when you grow your hair. I love it like that. Here is a present, a tight black dress. No one can touch you. It would look better if you lost some weight. Salads are not only nutritious, they *slenderise*. Hold me, you know how my heart beats baby. I want seven girls who look just like you, bitch. Why were you looking at him you slut you make me sick, don't look at me. I'm sorry. I didn't mean to hurt you. I'd never hurt you, not my princess. You're stupid if you think that. Why did I go after a stupid ugly girl? You'd better write this down. Fat Ugly Stupid Bitch. In that order. I'll break your fucking arm. Watch your back. Oh oh oh oh oh I'm so sad, don't leave me, I made a mistake. No one ever loved me, not even my mother. Only you. I could have anyone I want. And I want you. Right here. Who makes you hot? That's right. Don't you ever forget it. You were a worthless piece of trash when I met you, get down on your knees. I have a knife. I love you so much I'll use it on myself. They don't mean anything, you're my *wife*. I made a vow, and I meant it, you sleeping and the sun, don't leave me! Why can't it be easy? Just do what I say and shut up I SAID SHUT UP YOU WHORE, you're sleeping in the basement. Where the ghosts are OOOOOOOOOOOOO they're coming for you. You can't even cook, I get hard just looking at you. Let me make you a nice dinner, you look tired. Who are you calling? Eat shit, I'm serious. Eat this shit like you like it and lick your lips, tell me it's the best shit you ever ate, better than your last boyfriend. He's dead, you're all dead. My whole life, no one ever cared. No one but you, look at me, LOOK AT ME. I'm crying, I'm crying for you. Write me a letter and tell me I'm the only one you love. I'm saving all your letters and I'll turn them into songs, hold me. Give me the flashlight. You know what I'm going to do, you asked for it. The glass end breaks as it smashes my face, he beats me until he's tired. This time I have to go to the hospital. My eyes are bleeding, I can't see. I fell. My dog jumped on me and I fell. I need to get back home. You don't understand, he's all alone. Is how it begins and ends.

46. Television

Paul. You stud. Keeping one woman true to you, jealous of her even, while chasing everything in sight. Sending them letters and toys, how much you love them. Love is one part of who you are: it's what you need. To extort love from others, fidelity, silence. I love you Paul, I really do.

It must be love because you are all I think about, and, like you, I require silence. And devotion.

I try to watch a lot more television, knowing that this is what you do. Two weeks ago, I saw the woman who loves the multiple murderer Henry Lee Lucas (who is slated for execution this March) on Jerry Springer.

Jerry and the audience were appalled by her. The two expert witnesses claimed she had a Florence Nightingale complex. Jerry yelled at her: He's a Killer! What is Wrong with you!

She seemed numb, and kept repeating, Henry loves me.

Lucas was seen on a monitor, live from prison. He said that people treated her badly on the outside.

In his final thought, Jerry said that some women just like to live on the edge.

I felt he was getting at something: Your sexuality inflamed, a sex-slayer just slays you. He lets you live, and you are like Snow White (delicately coughing up the poisoned apple) or the hottest trick in town, or, the one who removed the thorn, gently, from the lion's paw.

She seemed crazy and I liked her. Stonewalled, quiet in the white noise of reason.

On the edge of something. A bold world view:

Q: What if Lucas got out and murdered your teenage daughter?
A: We'd have to cross that bridge when we came to it.

We are crossing the bridge Paul, hand in hand. I may tell you how gorgeous the moon looks tonight. I may have been lying to you all along: the footing is treacherous, the water below is cold and black. It seems very far away.

I don't understand any of you

蘇軾和王安石進行
辯論，但神宗卻支持王
安石的新創。

秦二世還將獻議的人
斬首示眾。秦二世殘暴無
道，使秦朝遭致滅亡。

宋朝時候有個讀書
人，名字叫做孫山。

有一天，他
們在城中看見一
張舉行鄉試的告
示，就去考鄉試
人。

Henry is innocent

豈料他還沒有聽完，便
搖頭不已，表示不聽了。

Henry loves me

有一天，漢文帝
談治理老百姓的方法，

Personne, personne n'avait le droit
de pleurer sur elle.

蘇軾在黄州一處叫
束坡的地方建了房子，
所以他又叫蘇東坡。

47. HOCKEY

Thinking of my brother this gray Tuesday   of monkeys
I saw in Granby Zoo   visitors throwing garbage at them.
They lowered their heads   In Montréal

I was nine or so   your age

your brother watched hockey with you then   the Saturday
Night overture   you followed the Philadelphia Flyers
a Broadstreet Bully   David   who was different
this made you angry and protective   liked Lafleur

His rookie card traded for five Leafs and kept in plastic

The *flower* you said but kept your mouth shut mostly
your brother sitting close to the screen   in awe   enraptured

It's Dave "The Hammer" Schultz and he's behind the cage
going in for a full body check   against the boards
you were playing with plastic figures   High-sticking his
Lafleur   calling for the medic

Your mouths working the dusty pink O-Pee-Chee gum
Piles of wax paper   knee-pads   little white jock-straps

He liked Lafleur's imagination, his creative plays
You preferred the anterior action   taped knuckles
and wrists   jersey tied to hockey pants   vaselined eyes
and cheeks   gloves tailored to be thrown off for a fight

the sound that ribs make when they break
the slash of the puck hitting the twine

You drifted away from David   following the trajectory
of the Enforcer (broken hotel room   mouth frothing
cardiac arrest   the police standing on your chest
like game-hunters)

He came to your trial once   speaking to no one
he has never spoken   My brother and I at the zoo
I want to join the others   I want to hurt them
he pulls back my hands

His pragmatism and love   for what is contained yet never
ceases   to be inventive and somehow surprising

flowers that emerge from slits in concrete   Assists
within the rules of the game

There is your own brother   who watches   as your breath
mists the penalty box   head up   protecting himself

48. Snuff

Paul O for goodness' sake. What do you expect me to do?
— Janice Galloway, *The Trick is to Keep Breathing*

When the police and forensic specialists combed your house in the summer of 1994, they found very little trace evidence. They did recover the following:

A square of carpet
Black paint
A receipt for cement
A blood-stained blanket.

They were looking for video tapes, the six 8mm tapes that Karla had tried to find as well. They knew your profile, that you didn't like to let anything go. Look under the ceiling potlight, you later told your lawyer Ken Murray. Retrieve the tapes and do not watch them. He eventually turned them over to the Crown team, but by then it was too late. Homolka had cut her deal: they couldn't prosecute without her.

Me   KARLA'S DEAL
Paul   long silence
Me   Paul, Karla's deal

Which brings us here, we are coming to an end. My anger still at large. When I think of injustice: the Scarborough Rape Task Force retrieving your DNA long ago, and never calling you back in. *Whatever I can do to help, officers.* You smiled disarmingly: *It's not me.*
    Your lawyer, who followed your orders: YES SIR I HAVE THE TAPES SIR!
    Karla's lawyer, who cut a sweetheart deal over Blushing Apples and *café au lait* (Thank you, everything is — *parfait*).
    Your two-faced wife — examining her horse-and-carriage wedding pictures with her psychiatrist, she said, you're right, I do look sad.

Christ it looks like a funeral.

The drugs aren't working: please set up an IV not an IM of APODI-AZEPAM30MGBULBITAL100MG & show me my cards:

Love

I'm trying to say something. Listen, there are different perspectives, ways of interpreting your actions and trial. None of which have been explored since you are, in fact,

A PSYCHOPATH.

Your behaviours are pathological: consider someone like Jeffrey Dahmer, who murdered, mutilated, and devoured his victims because *he didn't want to let them go.*

The tokens that serial killers are known to take from their victims: an earring, a rose tattoo   cut from the black dahlia.

You would watch your tapes over and over, with pleasure, feeling sentimental: you loved these girls. And they loved you, they told you so.

I love you I love you I love you I love you I love you I love you I love you crying   I love you.

Paul   Tell me you love me
         Smile when you say it
         Keep telling me

I LOVE YOU

When rumours about the tapes began to circulate, it was suggested that you were making snuff films to sell on the black market. Karla: *I love snuffles.* A diminutive?

This rumour was dispelled when police viewed the tapes to find that they ended before the murders.

There was no evidence of tampering: the murders were not filmed.

Your private room was filled with newspaper detritus, accounts of your crimes; you kept a photograph of Tammy Homolka near you at all times; you would watch your tapes.

French and Mahaffy, alive again, their every movement documented.

Bathing, sampling perfume.   *That is a nice smell.*

If you killed these girls — *I didn't kill these girls* — this would have been recorded.

A souvenir, a remembrance. A testimony, like the rest of your *fucking reckless life.*

A phenomenon, like looping, where the dead return to life through the illusion of film.

Unlike Jean-Luc Godard

SYMPATHY FOR THE DEVIL

you are a filmmaker who insists on completion: you refer to a closed narrative as "a good film".

You were not afraid of discovery: They'll never catch me, you would boast. When interrogated you would place your palms together, thoughtfully: I was probably at home Officer. I'm working on a new rap album:

> *sometimes i be cool*
> *sometimes i be chilling*

Driven with a compulsive need to register the real, the actual. You could not have let this opportunity escape you:

To own a snuff box, secreted and valuable. That you could pull out after dinner and dip into, greedily, intoxicating yourself, the film of the stimulant, evident on your steepled fingers.

Sometimes I'll be killing.

Me	Do not invalidate my argument
Paul	Silence
Me	Some art is Impersonal

Paul   *The king was like a cucumber. They never suspected a thing.*
Me   Silence

POSTCARD: INTERLUDE

Who is Paul? What is he, that all our swains commend him?

49. NECROMANCY

You once visited a morgue secretly and were engrossed by the jars of embalming fluid, the steel instruments, the rigid blue bodies. You could say that I love the dead as I am necromancing you. I may have had an altar right beside me all along, my Latin beauty. To assist me in winning your heart: a table spread with white dolls, with cowrie-shell eyes and yarn lips. Chicken's feet, alligator heads, shelves of violet potions, and all of my *exvotos*. Wooden fetishes presented to me, gratefully. They are always hearts, cured of lovesickness, their complaints. A spiked cross, Spanish moss, a drum, my casketed snake, *Le Grande Zombi*. He died some time ago, though I hear him rattle and hiss when the ceremony begins. I have been cautioned against bad magic. Still, I produce my child, *Erzulie Red-Eyes*, and offer her a bowl of alcohol and pepper. And the goddess rises. To the call of revenge, a knife plunged in her chest to the hilt. I have made a doll of you. It wears the piece of your hair I have acquired, a frayed green thread. And each time a little girl suffers, I stick it with a pin. You will feel the sting, an obscure and terrible pain, each time. And on these occasions, I will feel it, three times harder, more piercingly than you.

Not to be on earth forever, only for a short while…
— Poem, King of Texcoco

50. List Poem

Paul's Summation

My rape kit and midnight: The Scarborough Bluffs
Karla throws cold water in my face, to cool me off, at the Howard Johnson's Motel
A little rat crawls through her hair in the pet store, it peeks out at me
The handcuffs she keeps by her bed
My Big Bad Businessman, she says. I'm your good little girl
The Niagara Gorge, where I kissed Tammy
Halothane, leaving a purple stain on her mouth
The ice ice I rattled into her drinks
Our pink house and barbeque: Kiss the Cook
The girls Karla brought home for me: bouquets
My video camera, learning to zoom in: extreme close-ups
Kneeling, she asks me. *Please don't let the blindfold slip*
Receipt: twelve bags of Kwik-Mix cement
Watching the sunrise in Hawaii that Karla taped for me, *sooo happy*
She looks at the map, confused, it is the wrong city, it is all wrong
One shoe, lost in the scuffle, left on a sign-post: pendant
Eternity, I like that
The rubber mallet Karla carried like a sceptre
Green Ribbon, the red ribbons I burned and all other evidence
Karla's eyes after I beat her: searchlights
Her immunity (*my heart's on fire, I love you, you little rat*)
My loss, wanting to die I have lost —
Discovery: please take care of my dog. I'm not talking
Plexiglass encloses me I am a Dangerous Offender
Karla's parole coming, I can watch her go
A railroad train, coming round the bend
The whistle blowing in the exercise yard
Too afraid to follow *I hang my head and cry*

51. REVELATION

And I saw a carapace of grass newly grown where terror had been, and the rain fell like the water of life, like the tears of the Lamb.

The children of Christ came and were safe from the Red Dragon who devoured the stars, who was cast out by the four angels. Their glory radiant in the heavens.

And I heard the groaning of the filthy and unjust, as they were scourged with fire and the venom of God's wrath: *Behold, I come quickly saith the Lord.*

Blessed is He who hath slain the woman of purple and scarlet, drunken with the blood of these children. And Her scarlet Beast; they are desolate and naked, burning.

And He that sat upon the throne said, Behold, I make all things new. And I saw the dogs and liars and murderers come again, starlets of the Woman clothed in the Sun.

They have begun anew, roaming the earth and their hunger is sharp. They slake this hunger on the untouched growth, they quench their thirst.

They add unto plagues and take of life freely. In sickness I turn to the Spirit who beholds us from His celestial city. Even so, I ask Him, come, Lord Jesus.

And await his Grace and Fury, imploring Him *come quickly.*

52. The Rest is Silence

Then I was inspired. Now I'm sad and tired.
— *Jesus Christ Superstar*

And I don't want you, and I don't need you.
— Marilyn Manson, *Antichrist Superstar*

I claim the term falsifier for myself, being an idea-thief and shuffler of second-hand concepts.
— Felix Guattari

August 27, 1997

Paul,

I feel remorse for writing you, but it's not personal. It is finished and I have to lay low for awhile. In Kingston. There is a hole in the ground there, a construction site. I saw it on a tour of the city, looked through the wooden planks. I'll hide there, or crawl into your cell with you: a Man and her Punk. Stop taking all the blankets — Pig. I want to watch *The Young & The Restless*; Nina has no idea that there are ten sticks of dynamite under the chair where she sits and cries: she has let herself go.

Karla has been moved to Joliette Prison, where she shares a cottage with seven other women. They carry their own keys to the units and share the cooking. At night they sing campfire songs and roast marshmallows, Someone's dying Lord, lalala.

I see her. In a picture in the newspaper. Walking through the grounds, a silver ring on her wedding finger. Her body is bloated and misshapen, she walks with another woman, the sun just —

(*I am not a lesbian!*, she said in court).

And I hear her angry voice break, I hear her
Whip the women, just around midnight.

Her mother wants what's best for her and so do I. Goodnight, sweet princess, Wretched queen, adieu!

I'm a liar Paul; I have lied to you all along. Some of this is true. I could draw a line:

Everything above this line is true   Everything above this line is false

I am disassembling, my motives and methodology eroding. There is disarray. As I unpack all the books and notes, and newspaper and magazine clippings from the tall wooden box beside me. I glance at headlines: Deal with the Devil; Holiday at Homolka's House; Bernardo's Fate Still up to Jurors; Burn in Hell, You Bastard. And at books stacked haphazardly together: Othello, Rage of Angels, Karla's Web.

Looking at Frank Davey's book makes me wish that I could draw thick black lines through all of my letters, leaving one phrase: I'm sorry —

That I was able to talk to you about everything I wanted to say, and you did not scare me. That generally, after surrounding you, with bright little flags, I never found you on the map.

That I dreamed of you, long ago. You were covered in blood and you moved toward me. I asked you to let me wash the blood from your beautiful face.

I am taking this face down now, from where it has been stuck since last August. Staring, right in front of me. Next to pictures of my grandmother, my mother, my father reading me a story.

I am lying in bed with the blankets pulled up to my eyes, my head turned away.

My father tells me now that I was an impatient child, he read too slowly. That I asked what happened after, after the story was finished.

He is a reserved man. But when he reads about people like you, his face collapses. He is quiet and sorrowful, when little girls are hurt.

Tammy, Leslie, and Kristen would have been in their twenties now. The age I stopped talking to my father about anything of any consequence. Running wild, without reservation. Reading, very quickly. Daring to dream of villains, living to this point.

Sybiline, I have borrowed voices, spoken through others. To recover, what is unsaid. Speaking (of) your silence and treachery:
Demand me nothing: what you know, you know; From this time forth I never will speak word.
I know what you have done, and it is finished.

Sibyl, what do you want?

(The *Satyricon* of Petronius via T.S. Eliot) A thief, we are as thick as thieves.
My papers, trashed, the useless fossils that gather dust in the basements of museums.
Your eyes that I loved so much, banished.
        (Barnardo: See, it stalks away.)
Like the mere thought of you, doing terrible things. Of myself, apprehending

the truth the whole truth.

In the Sun after all. You ruined everyone you touched, you are hated and I hate you.
And as an object of study, you are no longer valuable. Never to speak or dream of you again:

> The dead girls, pursued and followed, I leave to rest
> in the heavens as stars, the Pleiades, visible only to those
> whose eyes are unclouded, and pure.

The rest is silence.

Sincerely,

LEGEND/APPENDIX

The vermiform appendix is a long, narrow, worm-shaped tube...It is stated that the vermiform appendix tends to undergo obliteration as an involution change of a functionless organ.
— Gray's Anatomy

THE KILLERS

Paul Bernardo: Resident of Scarborough and Port Dalhousie. Serial rapist ("The Scarborough Rapist") and murderer. Arrested and charged, on February 18, 1993, with abduction, forcible confinement, aggravated sexual assault, one count of an indignity to a human body, and the murder of Kristen French and Leslie Mahaffy. Convicted on September 1, 1995, he has since been declared a Dangerous Offender (after confessing to multiple accounts of sexual assault, dating back to 1983). He is serving a life sentence in the Kingston Penitentiary, with no possibility of parole for 25 years. Family: Ken and Marilyn (parents), Debbie and David (sister and brother).

Karla Homolka: Resident of St. Catharines and Port Dalhousie. Bernardo's spouse, who on May 21, 1993 (represented by attorney George Walker), plea-bargained with the Ministry of the Attorney General for a reduced sentence in exchange for testimony regarding her participation in the French and Mahaffy murders. Tried separately in St. Catharines, she received two concurrent sentences of 12 years for manslaughter, and was eligible for parole in January 1997. She will not be tried for her role in the sexual assault of Jane Doe, an assault which she claimed she had forgotten. She served part of her sentence in Kingston's Prison for Women (P4W), and has since been transferred to Joliette Prison in Quebec. The details of her testimony and plea-bargaining were not known until Bernardo's trial, as a publication ban had been imposed, by Mr. Justice Francis Kovacs, in order to ensure Bernardo a fair trial.

The Victims

Tammy Lyn Homolka: Homolka's 16-year-old sister, who was drugged and raped by Bernardo and Homolka at the Homolka family household in St. Catharines on Christmas Eve, 1990. She died after aspirating her own vomit, and as a result of the alcohol, and drugs — Halcion and Halothane — administered to her by Homolka. Family: Dorothy and Karel (parents), Lori and Karla (sisters).

Leslie Erin Mahaffy: A 14-year-old girl from Burlington, abducted by Paul Bernardo on June 15, 1991, after attending a wake for friends who were killed in a car accident. Her dismembered body, encased in concrete blocks, was discovered by fishermen in Lake Gibson, St. Catharines, two weeks later. Family: Dan and Debbie (parents), Ryan (brother).

Kristen Dawn French: A 15-year-old girl from St. Catharines who was abducted by Bernardo and Homolka in the parking lot of the Grace Lutheran Church on April 16, 1992. Her naked body was discovered in a ditch in Burlington two weeks later; her hair had been cut off. Family: Donna and Doug French (parents).

Jane Doe: A teenage associate of Homolka's, whose 1991 drugging and rape, in the Bernardo's Port Dalhousie home, was orchestrated by Homolka.

Jane Doe (1-19): Bernardo's Scarborough rape victims.

THE LAW, POLICE, GEOGRAPHY

Team Bernardo: John Rosen, defence attorney, a high-profile Toronto criminal lawyer. Tony Bryant, co-counsel. Both were appointed after Ken Murray, defence attorney, and Carolyn MacDonald, Murray's co-defence counsel (who have since been charged with professional misconduct, obstruction of justice, and possession of child pornography), removed themselves from the case.

Team Homolka: George Walker, criminal lawyer who cut Homolka's plea-bargain at Toronto's *Auberge du Pommier* restaurant. Ray Houlahan, prosecutor, a Crown attorney based in St. Catharines. Named Queen's Counsel in 1981, he agreed to write to Corrections Canada and the National Parole Board, detailing Homolka's cooperation with the Crown.

Justices: Frances Kovacs, who presided over Homolka's 1993 trial in St. Catharines. Homolka pleaded guilty to two counts of manslaughter. Kovacs deemed Homolka's acts "monstrous and depraved"; however, she was not sentenced to life imprisonment as she had no criminal record; she offered a plea of guilty, and had cooperated fully with the law. Patrick Le Sage, an associate chief justice of the Ontario Court, general division. He presided over Paul Bernardo's 1995 trial; he has been a judge since 1975, and has served as a director of Crown attorneys for Ontario.

The Metro and Green Ribbon Task Force, headed by Inspector Vince Bevan, and assigned to the French and Mahaffy case; Scarborough Rape Task Force; Niagara Regional Police; Metro Sex Assault Squad; Centre For Forensic Sciences in Toronto; Scarborough Rapist Task Force.

Ontario: Toronto, Port Dalhousie, St. Catharines, Scarborough, Burlington, Kingston.

Quebec.

BIBLIOGRAPHY

Abrams, M.H. *A Glossary of Literary Terms*. Sixth Edition. Toronto: Harcourt Brace & Company, 1993.

Algebra: A Senior Course. Eds. P.A. Petrie et al. Toronto: The Copp Clark Publishing Co. Limited, 1946.

Aquinas, Thomas. In Sidney Sheldon's *Rage of Angels*. New York: Warner, 1980.

Bachelard, Gaston. *The Poetics of Space*. Transl. Maria Jolas. Boston: Beacon Press, 1969.

Barthes, Roland. *S/Z*. Transl. Richard Miller. New York: Farrar, Straus and Giroux, 1974.

Baudelaire, Charles. *Les Fleurs du Mal*. Transl. Richard Howard. Boston: David R. Godine, Publisher, Inc., 1983.

Baudrillard, Jean. *Simulations*. Transl. Paul Foss, Paul Patton and Philip Beitchman. New York: Semiotext(e), 1983.

Beckett, Samuel. *Waiting for Godot*. New York: Grove Press, 1982.

Benjamin, Walter. *Illuminations*. Transl. Harry Zohn. New York: Schocken Books, 1968.

Beowulf. New York: Norton, 1975.

Bernstein, Charles. *A Poetics*. Cambridge: Harvard UP, 1992.

Berryman, John. *The Dream Songs*. New York: Farrar, Straus and Giroux, 1981.

Blatchford, Christie. "Justice Gained, Innocence Lost". *The Toronto Sun*, Sept. 1, 1995.

— "The Cold, Cold Beauty of the Law". *The Toronto Sun*, Aug. 29, 1995.

— "Bernardo Untouched by the Terror". *The Toronto Sun*, Aug. 17, 1995.

— "Icy Bernardo Chills Soul". *The Toronto Sun*, Aug. 16, 1995.

— "Bizarre Horror of the Ordinary". *The Toronto Sun*, June 2, 1995.

Body Count. "Body Count's in the House". Written by Ice-T/Ernie C. Copyright 1992 Rhyme Syndicate Music.

— "KKK Bitch". Written by Ice-T/Ernie C. Copyright 1992 Rhyme Syndicate Music.

Bowles, Polly Peterson and Barbara Peterson Burwell. *Becoming a Beauty Queen*. New York: Prentice Hall, 1987.

Buonarroti, Michelangelo. In Albert Elsen's *The Purposes of Art*. Fourth Edition. Toronto: Holt, Rinehart and Wilson, 1981.

Burgess, Tony. "Blonde Van/Beige Camaro". Illustrations by Dominic Pirone. Copyright Burgess/Pirone, 1996.

Burnside, Scott and Alan Cairns. *Deadly Innocence*. New York: Warner Books, 1995.

— "Deadly Innocent". *The Toronto Sun*, Sept. 1, 1995.

Cairns, Alan. "Bernardo Slugged by Inmate". *The Toronto Sun*, Dec. 7, 1996.

Camus, Albert. *L'étranger*. Paris: *Editions Gallimard*, 1957.

Cash, Johnny. "Folsom Prison Blues" (Live). Written by Johnny Cash. Copyright Columbia/Legacy, 1967.

Cather, Willa. "Paul's Case". Reprinted in *38 Short Stories*. Second Edition. Ed. Michael Timko. New York: Knopf, 1979.

Causse, Rolande and Jacques le Scanff. *Le Grand Livre des Prénoms*. Paris: *Librarie Hachette*, 1972.

Cavell, Stanley. *The World Viewed*. Cambridge: Harvard UP, 1979.

Chatto, James. "The Bernardo Industry". *Toronto Life*. May, 1994. 51-58.

Chaucer, Geoffrey. *The Canterbury Tales*. London: J.M. Dent & Sons Ltd., 1984.

Cousteau, Jacques (With James Dugan). *The Living Sea*. New York: Harper & Row, 1963.

Crawford, Joan. As portrayed by Faye Dunaway in *Mommie Dearest*. Director: Frank Perry, 1981.

Davey, Frank. *Karla's Web*. Toronto: Viking, 1994.

Deleuze, Gilles. "Coldness and Cruelty". In *Masochism*. New York: Zone Books, 1989. 9-123.

Derrida, Jacques. *Writing and Difference*. Transl. Alan Bass. Chicago: Chicago UP, 1978.

Dick, Leslie. "Feminism, Writing, Postmodernism". In *From My Guy to Sci-Fi: Genre and Women's Writing in the Postmodern World*. Ed. Helen Carr. London: Pandora, 1989. 204-214.

Dick, Philip K. *Martian Time Slip*. New York: Ballantine, 1964.

Dickinson, Emily. *Final Harvest: Emily Dickinson's Poems*. Selected by Thomas A. Johnson. Toronto: Little, Brown and Company, 1961.

Donne, John. "Holy Sonnet 14". Reprinted in *The Norton Anthology of Poetry*. Fourth Edition. Eds. Margaret Ferguson, Mary Jo Salter, John Stallworthy. New York: Norton, 1996.

Doors, The. "Break on Through (To the Other Side)". Written and composed by Jim Morrison, Ray Manzarek, John Densmore and Robby Krieger. © 1967 Doors Music Company.

— "The End". Written and composed by Jim Morrison, Ray Manzarek, John Densmore and Robby Krieger. © 1967 Doors Music Company.

— "Back Door Man". Written by W. Dixon and C. Burnett. © Arc Music, BMI.

Eco, Umberto. *Semiotics and the Philosophy of Language*. Bloomington: Indiana UP, 1986.

Eliot, T.S. "The Waste Land". *Collected Poems:1909-1962*. Boston: Faber and Faber, 1963.

— "Preludes". *Collected Poems*.

Finkle, Derek. "The Current Affair Affair". *The Globe and Mail*, Dec. 4, 1993.

Foucault, Michel. *Madness and Civilization*. Transl. Richard Howard. New York: Random House, 1973.

Freud, Sigmund. *Case Histories I: 'Dora' and 'Little Hans'*. Transl. Alix and James Strachey. New York: Penguin, 1985.

Frost, Robert. "The Road Not Taken". Reprinted in *The Norton Anthology of Poetry*. Fourth Edition.

Galloway, Janice. *The Trick is to Keep Breathing*. Edinburgh: Polygon, 1989.

Genet, Jean. *The Miracle of the Rose*. Transl. Bernard Frechtman. New York: Grove Press, 1966.

Gray, Henry. *Gray's Anatomy*. Philadelphia: Running Press, 1974.

Guattari, Félix. *Chaosophy*. New York: Semiotext(e), 1995.

Hamilton, Edith. *Mythology*. New York: Penguin, 1989.

Harris, Thomas. *Red Dragon*. New York: Bantam, 1981.

Hawkes, Wendy. *1996 Oriental Horoscope*. Boca Raton: Globe Communications Corp., 1995.

Hole. "Good Sister/Bad Sister". Written by Hole. © 1991 Bad Sister Music BMI.

Holy Bible, The. Authorized King James Version. Toronto: Collins, 1975.

Irigaray, Luce. *This Sex Which Is Not One*. Transl. Catherine Porter, with Carolyn Burke. New York: Cornell UP, 1985.

James, Hilary. *The Little Book of Fortune Telling*. Boca Raton: Globe
    Communications Corp., 1996.
Jenish, D'Arcy. "Horror Stories: The Case Against Paul Bernardo".
    Maclean's, May 29, 1995. 14-17.
— "In His Own Defence". *Maclean's*, Aug.28, 1995. 36-40.
— "Paul Bernardo's Mystery Woman". *Maclean's*, Aug. 26, 1996. 12-13.
Joyce, James. *Finnegan's Wake*. New York: Viking, 1968.
Julian of Norwich. *A Book of Showings*. Reprinted in *The Norton
    Anthology of Literature by Women*. Eds. Sandra M. Gilbert and
    Susan Gubar. New York: Norton, 1985.
King of Texcoco. In A.P. Antippas's *A Brief History of Voodoo: Slavery
    and the Survival of the African Gods*. Copyright 1990, Hemb
    Concex.
Leach, Penelope. *Your Baby & Child: From Birth to Age Five*. New York:
    Knopf, 1989.
Led Zeppelin. "Stairway to Heaven". Written by Jimmy Page and Robert
    Plant. © Atlantic Recording Corporation, 1971.
— "Whole Lotta Love". Written by John Bonham, John Paul Jones, Jimmy
    Page and Robert Plant. © Atlantic Recording Corporation, 1969.
Leyton, Elliott. *Hunting Humans*. Toronto: McLelland & Stewart Inc.,
    1986.
Levi, Herbert W. and Lorna R. Levi. *Spiders and Their Kin*. New York:
    Golden Press, 1968.
Lewis, Jerry Lee. "Whole Lotta Shakin' Goin' On". Copyright Roy Hall.
    Sun Records, 1957.
Lorde, Audre. "Recreation". Reprinted in *The Norton Anthology of Poetry*.
    Third Edition Shorter. Eds. Alexander W. Allison et al.
    New York: Norton, 1983.
Lloyd Webber, Andrew and Tim Rice. "Gethsemane (I Only Want to
    Say)". Copyright 1970 by Leeds Music Ltd.
Lynette. "Like Never Before". *Lusty Letters*. November, 1995.
Mallarmé, Stéphane. *Igitur*. Transl. Jack Hirschman. Los Angeles: Press of
    the Pegacycle Lady, 1974.
Manson, Marilyn. "The Beautiful People". Written by Marilyn Manson and
    Twiggy Ramirez. © 1996 Interscope Records.

Milton, John. *Paradise Lost and Selected Poetry and Prose*. Toronto: Holt, Rinehart and Winston, 1951.

Nietzsche, Friedrich. *Beyond Good and Evil*. Transl. R.J. Hollingdale. New York: Penguin, 1981.

Pearson, Patricia. "Behind Every Successful Psychopath". *Saturday Night*, Oct. 1995. 50-63.

Pencil Puzzles and Word Games. Editor-in-Chief. Erica L. Rothstein. Dell, May, 1996.

Plath, Sylvia. *Collected Poems*. Ed. Ted Hughes. London: Faber and Faber, 1981.

Posey, Carl. (Illustrations Will Simpson). "Guy De Maupassant". In *The Big Book of Weirdos*. New York: Paradox Press, 1995. 78-81.

Pron, Nick. *Lethal Marriage*. Toronto: McLelland-Bantam Inc., 1995.

Rolling Stones, The. "Midnight Rambler (Live)". *Hot Rocks 1964-1971*. Written by Mick Jagger and Keith Richards. © ABKCO Music and Records, Inc., 1971.

Sacher-Masoch, Leopold Ritter von. *Venus in Furs*. In *Masochism*.

Sexton, Anne. *The Complete Poems*. Boston: Houghton Mifflin, 1981.

Shakespeare, William. *Hamlet*. The Complete Work of William Shakespeare. Cambridge: Cambridge UP, 1982.

— *Othello*. *The Complete Work*.

— *The Tempest*. *The Complete Work*.

— *The Two Gentlemen of Verona*. *The Complete Work*.

— "Sonnet 130". *The Complete Work*.

— "Sonnet 146". *The Complete Work*.

Sherring, Susan. "Bernardo Fantasy Detailed". *The Ottawa Sun*. Reprinted in *The Toronto Sun*, Oct. 23, 1996.

Sir Gawain and the Green Knight. Verse Transl. Marie Borroff. New York: Norton, 1967.

Spoto, Donald. *The Dark Side of Genius: The Life of Alfred Hitchcock*. Toronto: Little, Brown and Company, 1983.

Swenson, May. "Cardinal Ideograms". *New and Selected Things Taking Place*. Boston: Little Brown/Atlantic Monthly Press, 1978.

Tourneur, Cyril. *The Revenger's Tragedy*. In *Webster and Tourneur*. New York: Hill and Wang Inc., 1968.

Wafer, Jim. *The Taste of Blood*. Philadelphia: Pennsylvania UP, 1991.

Webster, John. *The Duchess of Malfi*. New York: Norton, 1995.
— *The White Devil*. In *Webster and Tourneur*.
Williams, Stephen. *Invisible Darkness*. Toronto: Little, Brown and
Company, 1996.
Williams, Tennessee. *A Streetcar Named Desire*. New York: New
Directions, 1980.
— *The Night of the Iguana*. In *Tennessee Williams: Three by Tennessee*. New
York: Signet, 1976.
Wood, Trish. Host: *The Fifth Estate*. (CBC). *Karla Homolka*. April, 1997.
Wyatt, Thomas. "Whoso List to Hunt". Reprinted in *The Norton
Anthology of Poetry*. Fourth Edition.
Zwolinski, Mark. *The Fight of His Life: The John Kordic Story*. Toronto:
Macmillan, 1995.

NOTES

Epigraphs
(A) good deal of the incidental symbolism...
T.S. Eliot, Notes on The Waste Land.

1. Fear
There is no news in fear...
Anne Sexton, "Imitations of Drowning". *The Complete Poems*.

(y)ou know the day divides the night...
The Doors, "Break on Through (To the Other Side)".

...they begin to contradict each other.
A woman of ill repute...
Silence is usually the preferable surrounding for the reading of cards.
Hillary James, *The Little Book of Fortune Telling*.

*...the tiger's claw beneath the glove and inner savagery. This dangerous and beau-
tiful cat woman...beast of prey...*
Friedrich Nietzsche, *Beyond Good and Evil*.

Commes d'autres par la tendressse…
Charles Baudelaire, "Le Revenant".

…dark realm…
Edith Hamilton (Describing Hades). *Mythology.*

Poor soul, the centre of my sinful earth
William Shakespeare, Sonnet 146.

…dislocation occurs when the arm is abducted…
Henry Gray, *Gray's Anatomy.*

And make his eyes like comets shine through blood.
When the bad bleeds, then is the tragedy good.
Cyril Tourneur, *The Revenger's Tragedy.* Act III, Scene V. (Vendice).

…avec des cris de haine.
Albert Camus, *L'étranger.*

My mistress's eyes…
William Shakespeare, "Sonnet 130".

Illuminations.
Walter Benjamin, *Illuminations.*

…giving his concentration and energy to acquiring some other skill.
Penelope Leach, *Your Baby & Child: From Birth to Age Five.*

3. At the Courthouse Last July
Cardinal Ideograms
May Swenson, "Cardinal Ideograms". *New and Selected Things Taking Place.*

4. The Drugs That Killed Tammy
In a cowslip's bell I lie.
William Shakespeare, *The Tempest.* Act V, Scene I. (Ariel).

5. By Any Other Name

De ses yeux et de ses mains...
Causse, Rolande and Jacques le Scanff, *Le Grand Livre des Prénoms*.

For it is written, I will destroy the wisdom of the wise...
The Holy Bible, "The First Epistle of Paul the Apostle to the Corinthians". I:19.

6. Jason Lives

With the other masquerades...
T.S. Eliot, "Preludes". *Collected Poems*.

...a monstrous sexual predator...
Trish Wood

...mutinous winds...
William Shakespeare, *The Tempest*. Act V, Scene I. (Prospero).

postcard: Pencil Puzzles and Word Games

This postcard is indebted to some of the paradigms used in (Dell) *Pencil Puzzles and Word Games Magazine*.

7. The Night of the Iguana

O Courage, could you not as well...
Tennessee Williams, *The Night of the Iguana*. Act III. (Nonno).

8. Pornography

I recognized him immediately. I'd always wondered if I would... My husband can never know...
Lynette, "Like Never Before".

9. The Scarborough Rapist (two)

I'm called a hit and run raper, in anger.
The Rolling Stones. "The Midnight Rambler (Live)".

and she is chilly & lost... Song 117.
...stupid questions asked me/move me to homicide — Song 118.
...I'll take an ax/to her inability... Song 271.
John Berryman, *The Dream Songs*.

11.1. Leslie's Notebook
I'll never look into your eyes again.
The Doors, "The End".

12. The Green Knight
Much of this letter re-tells *and quotes from* the Ricardian poem *Sir Gawain and the Green Knight*.

13. Sex Trial (The Ghost-Tantric Orgasm)
...embryological relic...
Luce Irigaray, *This Sex Which Is Not One*

14. The Journalist and the Murderer
Christie loves Paul
Graffito, Jello Bar, Montréal.

15. Pretty Thoughts
The image of *pretty thoughts* collected in a jar is derived from Carl Posey's account, "Guy De Maupassant".

16. Three Killers
Now let's git real low one time...I said shake, baby, shake...Come on over, baby; baby you can't go wrong.
Jerry Lee Lewis, "Whole Lotta Shakin' Goin' On".

17. A Poetics
I'll be the biggest scar in your side...
Hole, "Good Sister/Bad Sister".

I will kiss you when
I cut up a dozen new men...
Anne Sexton, "Again and Again and Again". *The Complete Poems.*

18. Miracle of the Rose
...beauty is the projection of ugliness...
Jean Genet, *Miracle of the Rose.*

Nor ever chaste, except you ravish me.
John Donne, "Holy Sonnet 14".

19. Two Boy Scouts
...a contour against the void.
Michel Foucault, *Madness and Civilization.*

20. Karla's Suicide Desire
Dying
Is an art, like everything else.
I do it exceptionally well.

I do it so it feels like hell.
...
It's easy enough to do it in a cell.
Sylvia Plath, "Lady Lazarus".

Maids, the long royal lady.
...
They taste the spring.
Sylvia Plath, "Wintering". *Collected Poems.*

postcard: Witness for the Prosecution
This postcard consists, almost entirely, of assorted found-text from Polly Peterson Bowles and Barbara Peterson Burwell's *How to Become a Beauty Queen.*

22. Lovebirds
They know I can't move a finger, so I'll just sit here quietly in case...
Norman Bates, Psycho. In Donald Spoto's *The Dark Side of Genius: The Life of Alfred Hitchcock*.

24. The Grand Illusion
Grand Illusion *is about the illusion of borders...*
Stanley Cavell, *The World Viewed*.

26. Paul's Current Affair
David with the sling, I with the bow, Michelangelo.
One who possesses such beauty that none may confine its spirit.
Michelangelo, In Albert Elson's *Purposes of Art*

29. The Little Girls Understand
Yes there are two paths you can go by...
...our shadows taller than our souls...
Jimmy Page and Robert Plant, "Stairway to Heaven".

There's a certain Slant of light,
Emily Dickinson, "There's a certain Slant of light" (258). *Final Harvest*.

30. The Revenger
...man hot and vicious!
Cyril Tourneur, *The Revenger's Tragedy*. Act I, Scene I. (Vendice).

Cover her face; mine eyes dazzle: she died young.
John Webster, *The Duchess of Malfi*. Act IV, Scene II. (Ferdinand).

A very fine religion!
Cyril Tourneur, *The Revenger's Tragedy*. Act I, Scene III. (Vendice).

I'll stick my knife right down your throat baby, and it hurts.
The Rolling Stones, "Midnight Rambler (Live)".

31. Algebra
The attraction between two objects varies inversely…
Algebra: A Senior Course.

32. Found Poem (2)
Save yourself. Kill them all.
Thomas Harris, *Red Dragon.*

34. Whoso List to Hunt
…wild for to hold, though I seem tame.
Thomas Wyatt, "Whoso List to Hunt".

38. The Avenger
…in heat
Of that ambition bloodily rushed in,
Intending to depose…
Cyril Tourneur, *The Revenger's Tragedy.* Act II, Scene IV. (The Duke).

44. Argument
The structure of this letter is derived from the structure of Mallarmé's "Argument" (in *Igitur*).
The following words/phrases are Mallarmé's: *Four Pieces; About what follows; Prove; Dig into all that.*

45. En Attendant Linc
Come on come on make some noise.
Body Count, "Body Count's in the House".

We've had this date from the beginning!
Tennessee Williams, *A Streetcar Named Desire.* Scene Ten. (Stanley).

Death…The opposite is desire.
Tennessee Williams, *A Streetcar Named Desire.* Scene Nine. (Blanche).

46. Television
Personne, personne n'avait le droit de pleurer sur elle.
Albert Camus, *L'étranger*.

postcard: Interlude
This text alters the following lines of Shakepeare's "Silvia" song:

Who is Silvia? What is she,
That all our swains commend her?
William Shakespeare, *The Two Gentlemen of Verona*. Song: Act IV, Scene I.

50. List Poem
...I hang my head and cry.
Johnny Cash, "Folsom Prison Blues".

51. Revelation
This Revelation is modelled after *The Revelation of St. John the Divine*. The following images appear in the biblical text: the Lamb, the red dragon, the four angels, *the woman clothed with the sun* (12:1), and the woman dressed in scarlet and purple. The following phrase appears as well: *...Behold, I come quickly...* (22:7).

Hear him whip the women just around midnight.
— The Rolling Stones, "Brown Sugar". *Hot Rocks 1964-1971*.

52. The Rest is Silence
Wretched queen, adieu!
William Shakespeare, *Hamlet*. Act V, Scene II. (Hamlet).

Demand me nothing: what you know, you know...
William Shakespeare, *Othello*. Act V, Scene II. (Iago).

Sibyl, what do you want?
T.S. Eliot. Epigraph to "The Waste Land".

See, it stalks away.
William Shakespeare, *Hamlet*. Act I, Scene I. (Barnardo).

...the rest is silence.
William Shakespeare, *Hamlet*. Act V, Scene II. (Hamlet).

Acknowledgements

I would like to acknowledge the following writers, whose work greatly assisted my own research and trial-observations: Nick Pron; Scott Burnside and Alan Cairns, particularly for their work on "Julie" and Spike; and Stephen Williams.

For their coverage of the Paul Bernardo trial, I am indebted to *Maclean's* Magazine, *The Globe and Mail, The Toronto Star,* and *The Toronto Sun* (the reporting of Christie Blatchford, D'Arcy Jenish, and Rosie Di Manno was especially useful).

I also wish to acknowledge Frank Sinatra's "Summer Wind"; Michael McClure's poem "Ghost Tantras"; The Velvet Underground and Al Green; Professor Ross Arthur, for his exceptional reading of "Sir Gawain and the Green Knight"; Tony Burgess and Dominic Pirone, for their writing and artwork (respectively); George Murray, for his fearlessness; and *The Toronto Sun,* for their sensational headlines, specifically, "The Drugs That Killed Tammy."

And I wish to thank the following people, who read and discussed this manuscript with me: Tony Burgess, James Crosbie, and Mary Crosbie.

Many thanks also to Patrick Crean, for advice tendered; and, for their friendship and comments, Charlotte Vale Allen, Diana Bryden, Rex Kay, Ziggy Lorenc, Liz Renzetti, Leslie Sanders, Ira Silverberg, Michael Turner (of the *bold world view*), David Trinidad (my *pretty one*), R.M. Vaughan, and Rinaldo Walcott.

Finally, thanks to Mike O'Connor, fellow-insomniac and publisher supreme,

and to Michael Holmes, with infinite gratitude, respect, and love.

photo by Ian Crysler

Lynn Crosbie is a cultural critic, the author of three books of poetry — *Miss Pamela's Mercy*, *VillainElle*, and *Pearl* — and the editor of *The Girl Wants To* and *Click*. She lives in Toronto, and has a PhD in English literature.